I0555765

Published by Gracie Dancer LLC
www.rldonovan.com

Printed in the United States of America

Cover Design and Photography by Heather McCain

Website update by Brian Wetjen

ISBN 978 1 943976 06 5 Print
ISBN 978 1 943976 07 2 E-Pub

First Edition

DEDICATION

To my husband Joe, who makes all things possible.

ACKNOWLEDGEMENT

To Dominique for working tirelessly to ensure that this book is a realistic portrayal of the ski racing industry and skiing in Switzerland. Working with Dominique has been an awesome experience. I am really going to miss our video meetings (where we laughed virtually non-stop - but still got so much done) and Dominique's editorial comments that 1/always made it better, 2/always made me feel good and 3/almost always made me laugh.

To Laura Spaulding, whose ninja skills in searching ancestry helped me far more than any site or expert that we consulted

.

To Barb Lerouge for giving me the idea for my title.

To Punkie Skinner for her exceptional editing and proofing skills

IN MEMORY

Of Gloria Irene Janssen (Leemann) (Knak) Mom, the lessons you taught me are far too many to count. The laughter we shared together will fill my soul forever. Thank you for instilling in me the confidence to accomplish things I never could have imagined and for making sure I never lost an ounce of humility.

And of three remarkable women; Natalie Grasso Corbo, Janet Demarest Catarino and Bonnie McCord Woods who left me to fend for myself far too soon, but who all left an indelible mark in shaping my character and my personal brand. In this age of acknowledging women's excellence, these women are unequalled in their contributions to family, friends and the world at large.

Forward
By Dominique Gisin

During my time as an active athlete, it was always important for me to connect with my fanbase and the whole ski-crazy family in general. Maybe sometimes I lost some energy with this approach, but in many cases wonderful meetings occurred and long-lasting connections and even friendships developed.

I met incredible people on my journey and Robin and Joe are definitely an unexpected encounter (who even watches alpine skiing in the US at 4 o'clock in the morning ;) and just lovely and inspiring folks to spend time with.

As a book enthusiast, I cannot thank Robin enough for the trust she gave me from the very beginning of this collaboration. It was an immense pleasure to witness this book unfold and an honor to contribute just a tiny bit of perspective from within the ski-crazy world.

In the making of this book we talked a lot about my grandpa „Opa" and I want to dedicate my little contribution in this book to him in memory of all the crazy skiing days in the rain and fog and snow, he was the base of my values and ski fanatism and it would be a pleasure if this book would inspire some people around the globe to go out there and hit the slopes.

Disclaimer

This story is totally made up; except for the parts that are completely true.

[Chapter One]

Thump, thump. I wake and stretch lazily. It's a beautiful morning and Frank and Ellie are furiously wrestling for the privilege of greeting me first. I gather both in my arms – now the struggle is for who can first obtain freedom. In a flash they are off the bed and out the door again. On to their next conquest.

Since retiring I love waking up. No alarm, apart from the French Bully attack, no clocks, and no tripping over slippers in the dark trying not to wake Jon and the dogs.

I am Donna Leigh and these are the early days of retirement from my Omaha ad agency, Marcel. I am luxuriating in the knowledge that there's nothing pressing on my plate, as opposed to the last 45+ years of being slammed with client work and more recently also being neck deep in the 'too close for comfort' murders that seem to be occurring all around me.

The plan is to let my gut take me to the next phase of the journey and for now, my time is my own.

#####

Once again, Jon had awakened early and managed to get himself and the bulldogs out of bed and down the stairs without waking me. God bless the man! But what those two miscreants did after breakfast was another matter, and I knew instinctively that Jon must be on the treadmill hence providing the Frenchies the freedom to employ their special brand of wakeup call.

Sure enough, as is often the case, I found Jon on the treadmill jogging in place while watching Olympic contenders ski down a narrow and icy European course. No, this wasn't happening during the Olympics – Jon always amazes me as he enjoys watching these racing videos over and over again.

Always an avid (more like obsessive) skier and a huge fan of ski racing, Jon doesn't just watch the stats, he gets to know the individual skiers – to the extent that you can from observing their actions and comments about them when they're getting ready at the top, and their own comments when they've completed the race and viewed their results. At the top of his list are those with the best times along with the best comportment – how they interact with teammates and competitors is very telling. He has no tolerance for divas or arrogance of any kind. Sportsmanship and professionalism rank just as high as athletic achievement in Jon's book.

Since his own retirement, Jon's hobby has turned into something much more compelling, and as with so many things in Jon's world it all came about through happenstance.

One day Jon was commenting in a ski racing chat room. His comment received a persuasive response that left him stunned. The comment itself was simple enough, and in Jon's mind made an excellent point, but Jon was thunderstruck to realize that he was communicating directly with his favorite ski racer, the 2014 Olympic Downhill Gold Medalist from Switzerland, Dominique Gisin. It was an unimaginable thrill!

And it didn't end there. Over time, Dominique and Jon forged a strong friendship compelling him to study the ski racing industry with an even more in-depth zeal.

Prior to Jon's friendship with Dominique, we'd had a limited personal connection to anything Swiss. My paternal grandfather, Frank, had been Swiss. In fact, my maiden name, Leemann, was undoubtedly Swiss based on a genealogical chart that I had uncovered. But that was about it.

To Jon, it seemed as though this might be the time to take a closer look at my Swiss background. He's known that I've developed a burning desire to learn more about my heritage. Sadly, for so many Americans who are third and fourth generation in the states, we yearn for knowledge of our ancestors and their cultural history and are never able to truly satisfy that thirst for immersion in our own origins.

Jon had always been interested in genealogy. And when the DNA test confirmed that I am 33% Swiss – Jon combined his hobbies and began a deep dive for further Swiss connections.

[Chapter Two]

Having dispatched with exercise, morning ablutions and a light lunch for the pups and me, Jon almost never eats lunch, we loaded Frank and Ellie into the minivan and set off on our daily errands.

"It's kind of funny," I began, "that your hobby suddenly ties into my heritage."

How many times have I wished for more information about my ancestry and the furthest I'd ever taken the search for my Swiss roots was that one ill-fated drive through the hellacious Flüela Pass with Sparkey and Sue over a decade ago. I was so thrilled to be able to see the city of Davos along with some of the small Swiss villages and the lovely little hamlets tucked into each verdant valley that day. It's just too bad that the thrill of discovery was slightly overshadowed by the 'thrill' of near death!

We had embarked on a ski vacation in Innsbruck with our friends the Lanes, Sparkey and Sue. When I realized how close we were to the Swiss border I was determined to take a day to drive into Switzerland for a chance to set foot in the country that produced my grandfather's family.

We charted our course and set forth on a glorious, sunny day. With Jon driving and Sparkey (really Sue if you want the honest truth) navigating, this would be an exciting adventure. It seemed as though the Flüela Pass was the most direct route for this little excursion. Arriving at the entrance to the pass we saw a gate drawn across the entrance, but since it wasn't latched we forged ahead. We're American, it's what we do.

That trip occurred a few years before the internet would arrive on the scene so we all agreed that, since the gate was not latched and there was no one around for miles to translate, the wording on the sign must be a form of 'Welcome.' It wasn't until we were safely back in the states weeks later and Jon was regaling a German speaking colleague about our less than excellent adventure that we were to understand the import of our decision that day. As his associate threw back his head in great peals of laughter, he paused to give Jon the true meaning of the word 'geschlossen.'

"Nobody drives the Flüela Pass in the winter!" his colleague informed Jon. "It is far too dangerous. And by the way, outside of the U.S. the correct terminology is Flüelapass – one word."

Suffice it to say that once we had passed through that gate, the bulk of our day was spent as if on a treacherous and unrelenting roller coaster heading toward sudden death or at the very least, insanity.

Although the day was indeed magnificent, we were to quickly learn that high winds, especially in higher elevations, cause snow to blow across the road and form menacing ice. As frightening as that is on flat Wyoming highways, (where they close the roads on hilly areas or when it gets too windy and slippery) on the Flüelapass those icy passages are accompanied by constant and death defyingly steep hills matched by equally trauma inducing and heart palpitating pitched vales. Not to mention roads so narrow a chicken need take but one-half step to cross it, with nary a guardrail in sight.

By the time we stopped for lunch all four of us were sporting raw red throats from the near constant screaming.

We don't speak of it often, ever really. It is far too humiliating to be a fond memory. In fact, to this day we have never teased or mocked each other for our blatant and unrelenting cowardice – which is so not like us!

Every single one of us, to a person, spent the vast majority of that trip screaming like Goldilocks when Papa Bear gets home to the cottage. We bellowed with ear-piercing abandon, each time the car was in a descent, and we screamed just as shrilly for every ascent. I do not exaggerate when I say that our scream mechanisms were on autopilot and the only volume was high and higher.

With every barely perceptible slip of the tires our lives flashed in our minds with unrelenting fervor, simultaneously raising the din of screams to yet a higher pitch.

There were times during that car trip when we looked at each other, while shrieking in abject terror, each thinking 'my screams are an equal part of this cacophony and I am incapable of making them stop'! And if the sound of those screams were not terrifying enough – the look of abject fear upon each of our faces matched anything Stephen King could produce. We could find no solace in each other.

Conversation that day was limited to:

"Look at the lovely little village, the colors are just amAAARRRGGGGGG!!!"

And the like.

I cannot think of another day in my life where that level of intense fear dominated a seemingly endless car journey! And prior to that day, I would never have believed that an ascension in a car could be as bloodcurdlingly terrifying as a slippery, out of control descent. I would have been wrong.

When we started to see signs to pull over and put chains on our tires – I don't have to say that we've never had tire chains – we began to realize just how treacherous this never ending and never relenting Flüelapass could be.

We four hold an unbreakable bond that ties us like no shared bloodlines ever could.

Just thinking about that trip chilled my bones – and Jon was right there alongside me both physically and mentally.

"Don't remind me." Jon was looking a tad blanched, the memory still very real. "But on a more positive note, who knows, with some extra time and our friendship with Dominique, we may find ourselves spending some time in the land of your forefathers, just not without access to the latest German/American dictionary!"

I love an optimist!

Over time, Jon had come to realize that our death-defying jaunt through the road 'geschlossen' ('closed' to those who have not already checked the internet for its meaning) had left me filled with even more longing to connect with my ancestry. With all of my grandparents and my Dad and Uncle gone, I just didn't know where to begin.

Once back home from our chores, Jon buried himself in the endless and arduous task of tracking down my ancestors.

It was a slow and laborious process in which every new corner turned promised hope, only to be dashed by the subsequent response. At first, we knew only that my great grandfather's last name was Leemann. At every turn Jon was informed that he need only give them my great grandfather's first name to unlock a wealth of information.

What was most exasperating was the fact that I could put my own grandfather's (his son's) name into these search sites and get a ton of information on him, some of which I didn't already know, but to try and get anything on that next older generation, born in the 1850's was an insurmountable task.

On the bright side, Jon learned many things about how the Swiss culture views immigration, and how immigration back then functioned in such a way that exact information was not terribly relevant.

In speaking to several genealogy experts we learned 'it doesn't matter that you are positive of the spelling of your ancestor's last name, try looking for men with the last name of Lehman, Leaman, Leman or even Cleeman. We were also told that even though we were sure that my relatives had immigrated through New York, that perhaps it was really Canada. For someone with an orderly mind this haphazard means of obtaining information was nothing if not migraine inducing.

Ironically, after weeks of watching Jon search through the ancestry sites for my great grandfather's first name, I remembered that when my Dad died I had found a bag of old photos in his closet. Some were labeled on the back and some were anyone's guess. I had sat down with my Mom and we'd pieced together as many of the identities of the unknown faces as she could remember about my Dad's family. Once finished, I created an album that captured as much of the history as possible. Most of the photos featured shots of my paternal grandmother's Italian relatives, but there was one two by two photo of an elderly gentleman. On the back, in my father's handwriting it said "Grandpa Leemann, first name, Emil."

And then it all came back. I remembered as a small child hearing that my Dad, Emil, had been named for his mother's boss (a fact that caused endless laughter at family gatherings) and for his own grandfather. So, we finally had my great grandpa's name - no thanks to the ancestry geniuses. Jon and I were thrilled that we finally had the piece of information that we'd been told would unlock the mystery.

We were soon to learn how wrong that was.

After another pass through all the genealogy sites and chats with a few of the experts we were told "that's great, but we have to know precisely where in Switzerland your great grandfather was from before more information is forthcoming." Aaaaaarrrrgggghhhh!

In a nutshell, the experts recommend that the first thing you do when searching for an ancestor is to find all of your existing relatives and gather all the information you can, collectively. They even suggest running newspaper ads to find relatives you haven't already met.

When searching for Swiss ancestors it is important to know that the place of birth is less important than the place of citizenship. One library genealogy volunteer pulled up an Emil Leemann, but he and his wife were born in Germany. We quickly pointed out her error.

With unfailing stoicism, she retorted "it could also be the port from which they departed when heading for the U.S. – or Canada."

And still, at virtually every turn folks, including our librarian friend, were quick to say "are you sure it isn't Lehman." In fact, she even went so far as to say "even if it was spelled your way, it was probably misspelled any number of times along their journey."

So, what did we have? A surname we knew but were told to doubt. A first name that we had to find in our own photo album, a point of departure we were advised to question and a point of entry that was probably mistaken. Furthermore, if we found an area of origin within Switzerland, it could be any number of things but not necessarily the birthplace. Got it.

Curiouser and Curiouser.

We were absolutely sure it was Leemann and we were stubbornly sticking with it against all odds. That strategy paid off when, after many hours of searching and digging we found a ton of men and women with our exact spelling who hailed mostly from somewhere around Zurich or Basel-Landschaft. Admittedly, our spelling was relatively obscure, but dammit, it was there!

At this point in his explorations, Jon had narrowed my great grandfather's beginnings, with the help of our good friend and my former business partner, Laura, down to most probably the municipality of Binningen, Basel-Landschaft, which was still just a tad bit vague for our liking but so much better than what we'd had before. We were actually starting to make some progress thanks to Laura's ninja skills with public records.

In fact, based on several searches we had made ourselves we started to believe that great grandma's name was Theresa. But we knew nothing more. To our delight and astonishment, Laura was able to both confirm her first name and find her last name. It was Hofstetter. That was a huge breakthrough. We now knew her name, her date of birth, her date and place of emigration and were able to confirm that it was likely she had lived in the Basel region. We were really starting to get somewhere.

We were also pretty sure that great grandpa had a brother named Johan Adolf but who knew if knowledge of him would turn out to be the basis of more helpful findings on family members.

[Chapter 3]

Early the next morning, Dominique and Jon connected on a zoom call to touch base. They just loved chatting about the races in which Dominique and her sister, Michelle had participated. I think Jon was more excited about their wins than they were. And I was always so impressed when Jon shared his technical observations.

Dominique often agreed with Jon's assessments, albeit after the fact, and she always appreciated his input, even if, on occasion, he was politely suggesting that a slight change to her form would have improved her performance. I was mindful of other, far less acclaimed celebrities who would pretend to listen with their eyes glazed over and their attention anywhere else just waiting for the words of praise which were all they wanted to hear.

It was so impressive to see an Olympic Gold winner, who didn't need advice from anyone, listening so intently and discussing Jon's observations. She was never dismissive, nor did she manipulate the conversation for accolades.

Jon went on to mention that he had just rewatched her sister, Michelle win her second Olympic gold medal in the Alpine Combined. Each time he saw that win he became caught up in the sheer excitement generated by the event, even though Michelle's win broke the heart of her friend and teammate, who was another one of his favorites.

With Dominique's busy schedule it was hard to believe that she was, among so many other things, a dynamic and much sought after speaker as well as the author of several books, not to mention a commercial airline pilot. The fact that she took the time to chat with a fan/friend was always an inspiration to me.

In the ad business especially, you hear of so many celebrities at all levels of fame being rude and condescending to folks eager to have a word. I get that a selfie request in the middle of a gourmet meal can be grating – but don't these folks realize that without their fans there would be no fame?

As their conversation wound down, Dominique gave Jon a few additional tips to help him nail down details of my great grandparents. She seemed excited about helping us with our 'Swiss connection.'

"Who knows," Dominique commented, "maybe I have met some of Donna's ancestors already. Anything is possible."

With that thought they said their good-byes and I was left with a feeling of kinship that was becoming more and more meaningful as our friendship with Dominique and our quest for family progressed.

My best college friend and dormmate, Barbara Gray's mother was from Switzerland. Her mother, Lucretia Cola was born and lived in Cünter, Switzerland in the Albula district, speaking Romanche (that is Romansh in English or Rumantsch to the Swiss), until her Uncle funded her move to the U.S. when she was 21. A graceful and serenely elegant woman with an obviously high level of intelligence. From what I can recall of my college years, it was always a treat when Mrs. Fuchs came to collect or deposit Barb.

Spending time visiting relatives with her mother gave Barbara a strong connection with kin and culture – I was always a bit envious. She would send me spectacular postcards of breathtaking scenery and share stories of each and every one of her wonderful visits. In many ways, it was Barbara who instilled in me the first glimmer of a yearning to know more about my family's Swiss roots. That minute feeling of connection was powerful.

One of the pluses about Jon's pursuit of my ancestry was that I was able to connect more with both Barbara and my cousin, Howie (also Leemann) as we all tried to help Jon in his quest.

Howie, who sports a rigidly analytical, scientific brain shared in our frustration. For a man who prides himself on perpetual learning and microscopic detail – it baffled him that he didn't know his own great grandfather's name. Maybe if it had been a new strain of bacteria…but I digress.

It strikes me as amazing that we live our lives in and among relatives who have the key to unlock our ancestry and most of us wait until they are gone before starting to ask the simplest of questions about our own family history.

The more entrenched we became with the Swiss culture the more the desire to go and see what we were reading and talking about grew.

Since retirement, Jon and I had split our time between our home in Omaha and our ski house in Utah. And, of course, everything revolved around our French Bulldogs, Frank and Ellie.

In the past, the majority of our travel had centered around European ski trips, anniversary cruises to the Mediterranean, West Indies and other Caribbean locations. There had been a few overseas family get togethers (ironically, where all of the family gathered was from the U.S., but we still enjoyed our time in the land and culture of our ancestors – particularly France and Italy for me and Italy, Ireland and England for Jon).

Knowing how Jon's mind worked, he would be cogitating on a trip to Switzerland where we could finally meet Dominique in person, watch some race training, get some skiing in ourselves and possibly drive through the areas from which my family had most likely originated. Oh, and let's not forget finding an opportunity to try some of Switzerland's closely guarded wines.

[Chapter 4]

Not one to be easily daunted, Jon turned his ancestry search in another direction. He wanted to find out if it would be possible to trace the location of existing family members even with the scant information that we had.

After a few false starts, he became energized over the fact that this did indeed seem possible. Jon's virtual travels lead him on a merry chase around the mountainous and at times not so mountainous terrain of Switzerland. His digging unearthed a family by the name of Brunner, or when further refined, Bryner located in Basel-Landschaft (or BL). Since the family was living in the present, it was much easier to locate and tie them back to their distant relatives.

After several virtual jaunts within the county of BL, Jon settled on the village of Aesch where a family headed by a gentleman named Wilhelm Bryner resided. From what we could see, Mr. Bryner worked as a researcher in pharma and his wife, Greta, may have worked as an art instructor at one of the local schools.

Jon's next task was to locate contact information for Mr. (or Herr) Bryner and see if this connection was real.

Almost a week to the day after Jon discovered the Bryner family in Aesch, he was able to uncover an email address for Herr Bryner. We were so excited, Jon couldn't wait to share the news with Dominique. Her support had helped us on this factfinding journey, but what was even more exciting, was the fact that Dominique's Mother grew up in Pfeffingen, a little village near Aesch, and Dominique herself had spent a great deal of time there while growing up.

It was surreal. Finding this link had so many possibilities. It could enable us to meet some of my Swiss ancestors who could possibly help us find even more information about the origins of my family. And it gave us the sense of an even closer connection to Dominique. At the risk of sounding totally cliché, it really is a small world.

Once Jon shared our news with Dominique, she was delighted that there was a possible Aesch connection and she graciously offered to help us compose our initial email reaching out to Herr Bryner. Although it was probably safe to assume that he could read and speak English, observing cultural decorum right from the start would go a long way toward helping us develop the most positive relationship possible. It is amazing how minor cultural missteps can create tension and uncertainty – and Dominique knew we really wanted to get this right. So, we sent our rough draft to her.

As with many things, we had learned the importance of observing cultural protocol the hard way. One of the most vividly awkward examples of an inadvertent cultural faux pas that I recall was committed by our good friend Celia. Celia grew up in Malaga, Spain but was then living across the street from us in Connecticut. Back then she had organized a wine tasting group, for several friends, with a local wine merchant.

Our instructor decided to combine two of his groups for a tasting, one of the couples in the other group volunteered their brand-new home as the venue.

It was a beautiful and palatial home and several of us asked for a house tour. Our proud hostess was pleased to oblige.

After the tour we headed back to the wine tasting, Celia casually commented "your home is so beautiful, what did you pay for it?" Oh shit. I nearly choked as I caught the stunned looks from the others in the group magnified by the loud hacking sound made when the redhead near the back swallowed her gum. How had this never come up before? With all of the topics that Celia and I discussed I had never had the opportunity to explain that, in the U.S., we NEVER ask people what their house costs, or what they are paid and a whole host of other no no's regarding money that Celia, from Spain, had no way of knowing.

Our hostess graciously responded "way too much, to be honest."

Thankfully, Celia didn't press for more, which was very unlike her. Once alone I hastened to explain her faux pas in an attempt to stop her from trying to press our hostess for a more satisfactory response, but bless her heart she just shrugged. For Celia, her little blunder did not carry the shock that it had for the rest of us who were raised in a society in which asking for personal financial information was tantamount to asking someone to strip naked and dance around at the Macy's Thanksgiving Day parade. It just wasn't done!

Throughout the rest of the tasting I could hear a few little whispers about Celia and her colossally inappropriate question. I kept nervously turning to ensure that Celia had not heard the few shocked gasps or muted snickering. We did not need an international incident while tasting California reds! And trust me, had she heard we would have had one.

Our own group knew and understood Celia and all of her little peccadilloes, so to them it was just another wine tasting. To be honest, even without her untimely gaffe, our combined wine groups didn't generally fare particularly well, our two cultures were vastly different. We existed for pure fun and lacked a certain seriousness – in fact we lacked all seriousness, and their raison d'être was to pursue scholarly discourse. Although I can state with full accuracy that our group was always able to tell a red from a white.

I was pretty sure we wouldn't be invited back!

Suffice it to say, a seemingly small cultural faux pas can derail smooth relations. Not something we were willing to leave to chance with the important entrée to my Swiss relatives.

In crafting our rough draft for Dominique's critique I was certain of only one thing. Germanic speaking folks tend toward formality far more than we do in the U.S. So, I was sure that addressing our note to: Herr and Frau Bryner was precisely correct.

As I've come to learn over the years, while my cultural expertise did not result in a wrong approach, it was undoubtedly not the best. Dominique suggested we adjust the greeting to: 'Sehr geehrte Familie' to be formal, but to include the entire family.

Her corrections took me back to a few years ago when we hosted some young friends from France who wanted to polish their English to perfection. Hearing them refer to four-thirty as half past four always made me chuckle. Although technically not wrong, I hadn't heard the term 'Half past' since I listened to my grandmother when I was a little kid. That was when the realization hit me that foreign language courses are not always in touch with the latest evolutions of language and colloquial terms. And let's face it – language is constantly changing.

As we moved on through Dominique's suggestions, we soon learned that our attempt at sending a streamlined and to the point note was evidently the exact opposite of what our Swiss cousins would hope to see from us. Clearly, we had a lot to learn.

When we wrote: We would like to introduce ourselves to you, followed by our names, we were instructed by Dominique to "write something more about yourselves, for example where are you from…"

She approved of the paragraph where we talk about my great grandparents' names and agreed that my use of Frau instead of Fräulein (for my great grandmother's maiden name) was accurate, and that Fräulein is rarely used anymore (I had Googled that – I guess they substitute Fräulein with Frau similar to the way we substitute Miss with Ms. fearing it to be antiquated and even potentially offensive).

When it came to identifying Binningen as their probable place of origin, Dominique wanted us to again fill in details of our journey and how we'd reached that conclusion and to make sure to state why it matters to us – while absolutely mentioning our Swiss connection which would give them some trust in the sincerity of our reason for wanting to connect with them.

She went on to explain that "it is most unusual to approach someone you've never met via email.

"It can have the effect of making people feel exposed and they tend to "tense up." The best way to circumvent a serious breach of etiquette is to make sure to illustrate that you have a genuine personal interest and that you are not perpetrating some kind of scheme on them."

And finally, where we shared the fact that we believe we are related to them, Dominique suggested that we begin by asking them if they are aware of any ancestors who traveled by sea to reside in the U.S. She felt this approach would increase the likelihood of getting a more positive response. Apparently, the Swiss tend to respond better to a question than a statement.

Thank goodness we were smart enough to consult with Dominique. When you look at all the stupid and offensive, yet unwitting, blunders we had made, and blunders that could have created a tense and awkward connection, assuming they would even have bothered to respond. You may be thinking that the Swiss are an extremely sensitive and rigid people – but if you've ever witnessed how we Americans respond to a seemingly small gaffe (think Celia and the inappropriate financial question) – you'd know they are no different from us.

We made the recommended adjustments and hit send with confidence.

#####

A day or two after sending our email to Herr Bryner we received his animated reply. It seemed as though we were correct in our assessment about the professions of he and his wife. He implored us to call him Wilhelm or Will (possibly named after my great Uncle Wilhelm) and went on to enlighten us about his family, his wife Greta and their three children along with a bit about life in Aesch. Wilhelm also shared that the family had a vacation home in Engelberg where, as it happens, Dominique also has a home.

As thrilled as he seemed to be connected with a distant relative, he was at least that excited or more to know that the renowned Dominique Gisin was a personal friend of ours. Not surprising at all that they would have followed her career devotedly – she is a national hero.

What Will went on to explain was that, along with the whole family's love of the Olympics, in particular ski racing, their oldest daughter, 16 year-old Lyra, was determined to enter the world of ski racing herself and Dominique was unquestionably her hero. Having experienced an early disorder with a major impact on her physical ability, Lyra clung to Dominique's story of how she so successfully overcame some fairly serious injuries. The fact that we shared Dominique's interest in helping us communicate with Will and his family had oung Lyra so excited she could barely sleep at night.

[Chapter 5]

Jon's next conversation with Dominique provided some eye opening insights into her world.

"You know, Jon" Dominique started, "I love to see the huge number of young girls get so excited over a challenging sport, but in actuality, most have visions of standing on the podium, receiving the gold medal around their neck. Obviously, that is not everyone's reality."

"I see your point," Jon countered, "as the acknowledged expert it often falls on you to be the one to dampen someone's spirit by telling them that that particular lofty dream will only come true for a small percentage of competitors.

That's a bit like how virtually every college student, not on their way to medical school, thinks they want to work at an ad agency. It's always difficult for Donna when she finds herself having to rain on their parade. But she has learned that it is better to be honest up front rather than string them along, no matter how dispiriting that may be."

"That is exactly right, Jon. Once I have observed their abilities I have to make the call as to whether I will encourage them to devote their life to this dream or to just enjoy recreational skiing and amateur competition with their friends. It is quite daunting to have such an impact on someone's life path. Especially since I have been so fortunate in my own career. There are many cold-hearted experts who will chalk it up to managing expectations, but I know the pain that comes every time you feel that you may not achieve your dream and I cannot lightheartedly destroy a young person's passion.

"It is essential for me to be honest, but I also don't want to toy with a young person's self-image. There are two fairly major concerns with Lyra. 16 is quite old and not at all the best age to be entering events that are likely to lead her to a World Class ranking, and her past physical struggles could still prove challenging as she pushes herself further and further. Although, I have to admit, her ability to overcome significant physical challenges enables me to relate to her even more than all of our other commonalities combined. I fully understand the need and drive that she feels.

"While her family has given her the opportunity to ski in Engelberg, fairly often, all of the coaching that goes into the making of a World Class athlete has not yet begun outside of a few localized races in the Basel region, which is not the most competitive region. At this stage it would be impossible to judge if Lyra could be competitive in racing the kids who grew up in the alps. We have a great deal of ground to make up if she has any chance."

"Well, Dominique, please don't think that we want to put you in an uncomfortable position. We appreciate all the help you've given us in exploring Donna's ancestry. Working with Lyra is not your responsibility."

"Not at all, Jon. It will be my great pleasure to work with Lyra and assess her ability. I will help her evaluate her dream and determine whether or not she should pursue it. This IS my responsibility. This is one way in which I give back to the universe for all that has been given to me, and Jon, I do love a challenge."

He could see from Dominique's smile alone that she was all the way on board with getting Lyra whatever help she needed. And with Dominique on her side, Lyra had an advantage second to none. It struck Jon once again that he was honored to be friends with a true professional. But before he had a chance to respond, Dominique began to detail some of her thoughts about how best to move forward.

"Living in Aesch, Lyra does not have the best location in which to work on her racing skills. This is the same challenge that confronted me while visiting my Mother's family as a young girl. In fact, my Mom herself wanted very much to get into professional skiing because of her father's great love for the sport. They spent so many of their days in the snow for a girl growing up in the Basel region but it still was not enough to give her the intense training that a professional career requires.

That is why I was so pleased to hear that the Bryner family has a vacation home in Engelberg where I live. I can meet with her here when her family vacations and begin my assessment. After that point, assuming things progress as hoped, Engelberg will cease to be a vacation spot for the Bryners but will instead be more like their primary base of operations."

I couldn't help but think it was fate that Dominique and Lyra were both connected to Aesch and that they both currently had homes in Engelberg. But fate, as they say, can be a funny mistress.

Once Jon filled me in on his conversation with Dominique, we were both more reflective about the course we were pursuing. It's all fun and games to chase down your roots, but these were real people and their exposure to us could possibly have a major impact on their lives – and not necessarily for the better. It gave us pause for thought.

Before this reality check we had allowed ourselves visions of being at the Olympics, sometime down the road, and witnessing my relative on the podium. It's easy to get ahead of yourself. One thing we could agree on, however, young Lyra could not be in better hands. And, if it turned out that she was not the huge talent she had hoped, there would be no one better to let her down easy than Dominique, who genuinely understood the highs and lows of succeeding as an athlete.

It was time to get this party started.

[Chapter 6]

Over the course of the next several weeks, Jon and I spoke with Dominique on a few occasions. She had asked her relatives still living in Aesch what, if anything, they knew about this branch of the Bryner family to get a better feel for who she would be meeting in Engelberg.

"Luckily, I have enough family and friends in Aesch that their network extends throughout the village and they were able to paint a fairly precise picture for me."

"Anything I should be anxious about?" I asked with a nervous giggle.

"I don't see why there would be anything to make you anxious," Dominique countered quickly. "They seem like good people and it turns out that their daughter, Lyra, is kind of a local hero with her athletic abilities. A number of them have seen her ski and even race and their opinions tend to agree with that of the family. This makes me even more eager to check out this young prodigy, and make sure that she is pointed in the right direction for the most productive racing preparation."

Jon was nodding his head in agreement. He too knew the importance of getting right down to unparalleled training – both physically and mentally – in order to succeed in this most competitive of sports.

Years ago athletes would have snubbed the idea of including mental training for maximum impact. Today's successful athlete and coach understand that being able to maintain a high level of productivity mentally will make all the difference in the level of ability to which an athlete can perform. Physical ability is no longer enough. And many would argue that the superstars of old were able to succeed due to a natural ability to achieve that combination of cerebral nirvana plus emotional fortitude that is instilled in today's champions.

At lunchtime Jon and I found ourselves at a new eating spot. Over diet cokes and trendy salads, making sure mine included no products containing lactose, we chatted about our recent conversations with Dominique and shared our growing excitement. We couldn't wait for the Engelberg meeting.

"I only wish I could be there to see it," Jon observed.

"I know, I'm on pins and needles too," I replied, "it's almost like we're the ones getting ready to take on the world; it's so invigorating. The hell with all those people who said we would hate retirement and would start to feel dispassionate about things."

"Well, in fairness, they were trying to make sure we'd find a way to avoid that particular landmine. I'm guessing they were banking on the fact that we would succeed – with a slight push. And it seems pretty clear we have."

I could always count on Jon to find the positive in everything. So many people had assumed that we led an exciting and glamorous life for all those years we worked, and really we were just living our lives like everybody else.

It's difficult to explain to the majority of folks that owning a business as volatile as an ad agency isn't always the caviar and champagne life that they assume. But try to explain that to them and they just chalk it up to your being humble and go right on assuming that every day for you is a red carpet day. Once you've been around for a while they even start to refer to you as a legend.

The more I learned about Dominique and her remarkable career and successes, the more that made me laugh. Now she was a legend! Although she never made you feel that way when talking to her.

When Jon and I got back to the car we soon realized we would not be making a hasty exit. There was a growing crowd around our minivan as Ellie smiled and performed her many gymnastic moves for the audience. And once they realized Frank was sitting nearby watching his sister work the crowd, they were even more captivated.

Folks were laughing and clapping. She was drawing more and more attention. Cars trying to depart the parking lot were starting to jump the curb in an effort to move forward. We could see things were getting a bit tense at the edge of the crowd, but getting to the car to stop 'the show' would not be easy.

Once even the cars jumping the curb stopped moving the horns began to blow. And then someone was heard to yell,

"Ow, you ran over my foot you son of a…"

Jon and I knew it was only a matter of time before some do-gooder called the police. And sure enough, just as though we'd imagined it into being, a cruiser pulled up on the street.

One tall muscular gentleman in uniform accompanied by a uniformed woman who looked as though she was no stranger to the gym moved swiftly into the heart of the action. Within seconds they had sized up where the commotion had originated and were requesting the owners of the traveling circus come forward.

At the very moment that Jon and I were wishing to fade into the background we were forced to acknowledge that we were, in fact, the ring leaders.

Tall and muscular was about to begin the process of breaking things down. He had just opened his mouth to speak when Ellie suddenly launched into her next trick – several sudden quick bursts of the car horn.

Oh god, shades of our earlier generations of bulldogs. What was it about bulldogs and car horns. So many times over the years with our various bulldogs we were greeted in countless public places by folks warning us of the horn blowing and the lights flickering on and off. Bulldogs are characters and they love to make people laugh. You just have to take the good with the deeply embarrassing. We were once left a lovely note on our windshield when our bulldog, Gracie was sitting in the driver's seat with her head resting on the steering wheel. It read "I was having a very bad day and then I saw your lovely bulldog behind the wheel and it turned everything around." That note touched us so that we had it, and a photo of Gracie in driving mode, framed together. Needless to say, we never leave our babies in a car that is too hot or too cold.

By the looks of tall and muscular and his associate, Ellie's newfound maneuver did nothing to endear us to them.

Luckily, seeing the uniformed officers had an extremely calming effect on both Ellie's audience and the gridlocked drivers. Little by little they began to make their way away from our minivan and out of the parking lot. Since it was late enough to be between the lunch and dinner crowd things returned to normal surprisingly quickly with nary a word from the officers. I think that went a long way toward their slightly less antagonist looks our way. We did not, however, escape a moderately stern lecture, albeit, our fear levels were lessoned by the fact that both officers clearly had to work hard at not cracking up as Ellie's antics continued.

"Ma'am, Sir, we are going to suggest that you not park your vehicle in such a prominent place in a public parking lot, or you choose to leave the clown act at home," that punctuated with a giggle most unbecoming a civil servant.

"Yes, officers, we understand completely," both Jon and I uttered simultaneously.

This was not our first rodeo.

[Chapter 7]

Weeks had gone by and the much-anticipated meeting between Dominique and Lyra had been scheduled. The Bryners had planned a long weekend in Engelberg in order to give the pair time enough to talk and to ski.

Jon and I worked to keep our emotions in check. We exchanged a few more emails with my new cousin, Wilhelm, and we even received an especially sweet note from Lyra saying she was thrilled to meet her newest family members, even if only via email. She could not stress enough how appreciative she was that we were able to give her an introduction to Dominique.

We did our best to be upbeat and supportive toward Lyra and her whole family without giving them false expectations. In truth, we had no idea how things would actually transpire and we wanted to help manage their expectations, as well as our own, just in case. No pressure there!

As we reread Lyra's note, it occurred to us that her command of the English language was pretty much superior to our own. That was somewhat embarrassing, but it made sense that every generation of Swiss citizens would be that much more immersed in the English language than the last. Still, it was a bit much. Jon and I agreed that the day Lyra had to start correcting our English would not be a celebratory day – and it seemed inevitable based on what we'd read so far.

In one conversation with Dominique, she agreed that, once she had a handle on how things were shaping up with

Lyra, we should all have a Zoom call and really meet our new relatives. I didn't know what had me more excited!

The day had finally arrived. Jon and I both woke at 5 am knowing that Dominique was about to meet the Bryner family at The Tea Room, a remarkable reproduction of an English country tea room, squarely ensconced in the middle of a Swiss wonderland.

We knew it was silly as we quietly drank our coffee and envisaged the conversation at The Tea Room. Along with covetous thoughts of the delectable delicacies they were sharing, we couldn't help but picture ourselves in the setting amidst beautiful and timeless walls bedecked with classic English trim and painted in a deep, saturated green/blue, along with every possible version of that racing conversation. Not only would it play a crucial part in shaping the lives of the Bryners, especially Lyra, it would be an important part of our own future. There was no way that Jon would be related to a ski racing champion and not want to be there, up close and personal, for every important event.

We knew from talking to Dominique that this first meeting was not just a meet and greet, but an initial assessment of the attitudes of both Lyra and her whole family.

What she looked for in Lyra was a total dedication to her sport and a willingness to do whatever was necessary in order to exceed all expectations. From her family, a total commitment to support the life and work that would be critical to the success of their athlete. Every member of the family would have to understand that there would be many sacrifices before she could hope to attain a position as a top achiever. They would have to be Lyra's biggest fans helping with her logistic as well as her emotional needs. Anything less would hinder her success. What would be the point of assessing her athletic ability if the necessary drive was not evident in Lyra or her family?

"Donna let's go somewhere. This overthinking is driving me crazy," said Jon.

"You're right, I'm starting to lose it. We know we'll hear from Dominique, and probably even the Bryners as soon as they get a chance to fill us in."

So, Jon and I headed over to the Henry Doorly Zoo. It is an amazing zoo and usually ranks #1 in the country. After a stroll through the Lied Jungle, we headed over to the Scott Aquarium. We were hoping to get to the Desert Dome, but the afternoon had flown by and we needed to get home. You could wander around that zoo for a week and still might not get to see everything. There was so much to see and everything is absolutely enchanting.

Unlike the zoos of my youth where you walked by animals in cages, this zoo does an incredible job of recreating the natural environments of each animal. In the geodesic Desert Dome you are transported to the deserts of the world. You experience the surroundings and see how the animals live in their natural environment. It is a unique and amazing experience and is mesmerizing to us no matter how many times we go there.

It was the perfect way to occupy our minds until we were able to get the lowdown on the meeting. With a distraction like that there's far less strain on one's patience. Supporting our local zoo is a no brainer. We get to see all of these amazing animals in a simulated natural environment and we get to help support the phenomenal work this zoo does in conservation around the world. It is zoos of this caliber that keep many animals from extinction and so many folks are not aware of this.

On the way home we saw that Dominique had set up a call for first thing the next morning. We had also received emails from Wilhelm and Lyra.

"Read them to me, Donna."

I could see from Wilhelm's email that he was being cautiously optimistic. He acknowledged that he'd always held Dominique in high regard, but now more so than ever. Wilhelm was extremely impressed with the way the meeting had been conducted.

"It strikes me as so amusing that a meeting among Swiss people had to be orchestrated by a couple living in Nebraska. But from Dominique's earlier observations it was pretty clear that the Bryners would be way too timid to ever attempt such a meeting with her, through her various channels, without a formal entrée. Without our intervention it is improbable that

Lyra would ever have met Dominique and almost certain they wouldn't be working together."

"Maybe not timid so much as proper, unlike we Americans. Now what does Wilhelm have to say?"

So, I read:

"Dominique was wonderful with Lyra and our whole family. She was so gracious and was able to offer encouragement without making unrealistic promises for the future. Before this morning, we feared it would be impossible to manage Lyra's expectations. My wife and I are so grateful for everything you have all done for our family. We are indebted to you."

Lyra's note ran along the same lines, but her pent-up enthusiasm was undeniable.

"Cousin Jon and Cousin Donna, what you have done for me is beyond belief. Just to meet my idol was enough, but to think that I might get a chance to learn directly from her is more than my imagination can contain. I am about to explode from excitement."

By the end of the emails both Jon and I were struggling to contain a few stray tears.

[Chapter 8]

Our morning call with Dominique could not come soon enough. Up with the birds, neither Jon nor I could sleep waiting to see what, if any, next steps would be forthcoming. We drank our coffee in silent anticipation and were tempted to indulge in several refills but were smart enough to anticipate the bladder demands that would likely create should our call go long. We would let nothing cut Dominique's briefing short!

Finally, it was time for the call.

As we joined the Zoom call, Jon and I could see from her demeanor that Dominique must have good news.

"They are really a great family," she began, "and I think they have a good basic understanding of the level of immersion that would be necessary for every one of them. They said all the right things and they seemed to be genuine. Even Lyra's siblings were enthused about having their sister become an athletic star. She is that a bit already so they have some idea. And they have seen her fight through her physical disorder where they were right by her side to support and root for her. The seven-year old, Emma was so cute. She wants to be Lyra's manager. And the 12-year old, Leo clearly adores his older sibling. That is a very good start."

It was impressive how much Dominique was able to ascertain over a simple meal.

Jon wanted to know "did you sense any areas that might be problematic?"

"That's a good question," Dominique responded, "you know there is always going to be something. If I had to take an educated guess, I would say possibly the mother, Greta's teaching schedule could get in the way of some of the necessary activities. And even Leo and Emma might need to be tutored away from the home in order to get the necessary schooling at times when the family cannot be in Aesch. But I have seen many families alter their lifestyles completely once they have a child enter this demanding world."

"I suppose Greta might have to give up her job ultimately," I suggested, "unless they are able to make some concessions for her. Even Will could end up being away far too long to hang onto his own job."

This formed a bit of a dark cloud over our excitement. How would this family pay their bills and educate their kids with the sacrifices that might become necessary?

"Don't worry," Dominique laughed, "it will not be quite so dire as all that. We Swiss are extremely agreeable to alternative ways of supporting our young hopefuls. I am quite sure that Will's company will allow him the ability to work remotely when necessary, possibly from a location they have in Engelberg; you know so many things have changed since Covid and companies are giving employees so much more latitude. I know that has been happening in the states as well."

"Yes, that's absolutely true. And during Covid even teachers got to teach from home through video conferencing. It wasn't always easy but there was really no alternative. I do think schools prefer to have teachers be face-to-face with students these days so you're right, Greta's job could be a problem, especially as she's an art teacher. It has to be extremely difficult to teach such a visual topic without being face-to-face." I said.

"With Lyra as mature as she is, there is no reason why she would not be able to live in the family's Engelberg vacation home on her own and attend one of the 'Internat' schools. Even if things with Lyra really take off and Greta turns out to be uncomfortable with being a 1.5 hour car drive away from her eldest child, I would imagine the school will find a way to enable Greta to keep teaching."

"Or she could always take another, more flexible position." Jon added.

"I guess we won't solve all of their problems today." I chuckled, "Maybe we should stick to what's happening right now."

"Good point, Donna. I have set up a skiing session with Lyra for the day after tomorrow. I want to observe her for several hours. I need to get a feel for her skill, her daring, her instincts in various conditions, her ability to handle speed and her stamina. These will not all be determined in one session, but this should give me enough information to make some suggestions on training and counseling. I will be suggesting that she enter Schweizerische Sportmittelschule Engelberg, one of the three big sports schools of Switzerland, and the only one that is right here in town"

My heart went out to Lyra. So much would be determined in a few relatively short sessions.

"But don't worry Donna, I will not pronounce her "fit" or "unfit" after only a few observations. No one will know if she is, in fact, an 'Olympic' athlete until she has qualified and run numerous races. Until then, it can only be speculation at best."

I had to wonder, was she reading my mind now? I knew she had some remarkable skills but this was getting a little scary.

"Well, Dominique, if you can read the Bryner family and Lyra in as short a time as you've been able to read Donna, I think we'll get a pretty good indication fairly soon."

Now he was reading my mind too – am I really that easy?

We all had a bit of a laugh – albeit mine didn't quite reach their level of mirth as I pondered these two mind readers and how they seemed able to get in my head. I might not always be as amused by that. At any rate, I was sure about one thing, I was so grateful for everything Dominique was doing for my newfound family.

#####

It had been about two months since we'd been out to Utah. We liked to get out there for 2-3 weeks 4 or 5 times a year. As much as we enjoyed our lifestyle in Omaha, we adored the mountains, lakes and climate of our Utah home.

"We have two more dinner parties next weekend and then we're free for several weeks. Let's plan on heading out next Sunday if the weather holds up," said Jon.

"Works for me."

Another perk of retirement, I never have to check a work schedule before planning our trips out west. A few dinner parties and the occasional speaking engagement were all we need worry about. It felt so free compared to all those years of juggling schedules, meetings and even then bringing my phone and computer for the rogue emergency meeting which occurred quite frequently.

With the technology of today it was virtually impossible to leave work behind. And even if we could, strictly speaking, the technology habit was far too engrained in our psyches. However, if you own a business and think you can truly walk away for a week or more, you're just kidding yourself.

Even as a department head, I would sometimes come home from a vacation and walk into a series of landmines. Deals I had put to bed being restructured, and not in a good way. If a handful of dubious vendors know you're not there – they take their best shot at pulling the rug out from under you.

One example that still haunts me is a time when I had negotiated a deal for a media flight for a client. The sales rep decided to push me and tried to renege on some of his promises. I stood firm and he finally acknowledged our original agreement.

When I came back from vacation I was greeted by one of my planners who said "Oh, the rep called while you were out and said you had made a mistake on the paperwork. He asked me to just go ahead and change it, so I did."

I hit the roof. Far less at the planner who was just trying to be helpful, but I let the rep know in no uncertain terms that his little trick was not going to work. He grudgingly acknowledged that our paperwork would return to the original agreement - again.

"So, I took a shot." Was all he had to say for himself.

You always have to watch your back, in any business really. You get to work with some wonderful folks, but there are those few stinkers that try to get ahead at your expense – and they can come from anywhere.

[Chapter 9]

"Based on what I've seen of Lyra's skiing, I will gladly work with her to see where this will take us."

Jon and I were practically bursting at the seams.

"I can see that her basic skills are solid, and that she does not fear speed. It also appears as though she has good common sense and will not take risks that are unnecessary. I attempted to judge her capabilities under as many varied conditions as possible as we moved around the mountain searching for icy sections to test her carving skills. On a very sunny slope we were even able to find some soft springlike snow. I actually managed to find a small area with powder, so I had her take a few turns to ensure that she has a good feeling on skis and for all the various types of snow. Having such a wide range of altitude on our Engelberg slopes enables us to find varied conditions all on the same day. So far, I have been impressed with what I have seen. And my presence did not appear to make her nervous or affect her performance. I could see that she has the ability to improve on inputs (or suggestions) and implement them fairly quickly without having to stop to think and assess."

"That's incredible," Jon said, "It's better than we could have hoped."

I was too excited to talk – so I just made a few excited squealing sounds as I heard each thrilling comment. Don't judge me!

"So, Dominique, where do things go from here," Jon asked, "I don't mean to be pushy but I know there's never time to waste in terms of getting an athlete ready to compete."

"You are correct in your thinking, Jon. I have already prepared an initial schedule to begin the process immediately. First, her family will need to make arrangements so that she can live in Engelberg as her primary residence, and adapt to the sports school idea. We can begin some of the work while they are making these arrangements. We will start by having her race the athletes in training so that we are able to see her speed – we need to ascertain how fast she is. I would probably also work with her on weekends just to give her some "technical" extras and look at the whole systematic, for where she could improve and how I could support her in those areas. Possibly: physical training, mental training – but I imagine her early physical struggles would have made her exceptionally strong in this particular area – material setup, energy management, feeling for skis and snow, mindset, etc., but the full-on attack plan will begin once she is here full time."

"What kinds of things do you envision can get started immediately?" I asked.

"She can meet with a coach and a counselor right away, but even before that I will have her work with the training group in Engelberg to get a better assessment of her speed. Her family are very happy to make those trips as needed. And luckily, they already have a place to stay in Engelberg so that will help cut down on the traveling costs."

It seemed surreal. We'd just started poking around for my Swiss ancestors on a whim, mostly because of our friendship with Dominique. We never really thought we'd find relatives and we certainly never imagined that this discovery could help our newfound young cousin find her way to working with Dominique and possibly being a contender in the Swiss ski racing arena.

"You know, Dominique, we received an email from Lyra and one from her parents again," I added. "It's wonderful to see them all so committed to this goal, but for us, they all credit us with making this chance for Lyra possible. No pressure here, no pressure at all."

"Don't Americans say 'if you can't take the heat get out of the kitchen?' Dominique asked, "if you think the pressure on you is bad, think of how Lyra and her parents must feel as they turn their whole world upside down for one of their children."

She had me there.

We continued to correspond with the Bryner family and have regular Zoom calls with Dominique. We even had a Zoom call with Dominique and all of the Bryners. It gave us all a chance to see each other more than anything – there was a lot of energy and no real agenda – but it helped tighten our connection – at least it did for me. Short of a few very minor challenges things seemed to be moving along smoothly.

Dominique continued to assure us that the timing was on track and she even sent us a few videos of Lyra in some local races. Since Jon knows so much more about skiing and ski racing technique than I, he talked me through some of the key points that would potentially make Lyra a worthy contender.

Then one lovely morning just a few weeks later, Dominique told us she believed Lyra was at a point where it would be worthwhile for us to pay a visit to Switzerland so we could see our cousin race in person. Although Lyra's training was still at a relatively early stage, Dominique made the point that if we saw her in some of these local races now, we would be that much more appreciative of her capabilities as she advanced in her racing career.

"I think the added family support will be particularly helpful for Lyra. As a racer in training there is a great deal of pressure, but much more so in Lyra's case. Coming from Basel which does not typically connote racing excellence has racing fans intrigued and perhaps skeptical. Her modest amount of acclaim originates as much from her ability to overcome her early physical challenges, ones that would prevent most people from ever skiing much less racing, as it does from her decent performance on the racing slopes. Going from near constant pain and stiff and often unresponsive limbs to flying down a hill at stunning speeds, was something her fellow townsfolk would never take lightly. Suffice it to say that all eyes will be on her, far more than the average racing novice.

Jon could think of nothing else. He bought tickets and started packing a month before our flight was scheduled. The whole house became a staging zone for our trip to Switzerland. Naturally, Dominique, Will and Greta all had great suggestions to maximize our travel experience. They all volunteered their houses so that we wouldn't have to stay in a hotel. As tempting as that was, we did not want to intrude on their concentration at such a critical time. We finally agreed to stay in the rental flat of a friend of Dominique's. It was centrally located in Engelberg where we could be close to Dominique and our relatives both during races and Après ski.

[Chapter 10]

Right out of the gate, Jon started assailing me with facts about Engelberg to enhance my enthusiasm for our trip. It didn't matter that we had only planned a two-week stay, he was enamored of the fact that there is skiing in Engelberg from October through May. For Jon, that is nirvana. Although from what we've heard about skiing the slopes around Engelberg, they are not for the faint of heart. I knew for sure that I would be seeking slopes geared for cruising enjoyment and not ones requiring ultimate survival skills, and Jon wasn't about to pit his skills against these seasoned warriors – the Swiss – at least not right out of the gate (I know, I know, another pun).

"You know, Donna," he started, "Engelberg means 'mountain of the angels' because it is so incredibly perfect to look at and to watch the experts ski."

"You don't have to convince me, Jon, I'm already going."

"Yes, but I want you to be as excited as I am!"

"I get it, and I am excited. But trust me, there's little chance I'll get as excited as you are unless the trip provides a charming instructor with a cute butt, guaranteed to teach me how to ski those incredibly challenging Engelberg slopes with ease."

As expected, Jon rolled his eyes.

What Jon didn't realize was that I had been falling in love with the sheer charm and beauty of Engelberg from all of the photos on their website. It truly appeared to be a magical place and I couldn't wait to actually be there and experience all that it had to offer.

"They seem to compare the skiing and beauty in Engelberg with that of St. Anton, Austria. Do you remember that trip?"

"How could I forget?"

We had been walking back to the car at the end of our pleasurable day of skiing, with lovely wide runs and glorious scenery all around us, and we had just crossed over the railroad tracks when I heard a whistle. I looked down the tunnel and saw the lights of the train barreling down just as I turned my head to see a car stuck on the tracks. I heard a scream and then a crash as the train hit the car and spun it sideways with metal and glass crashing down all-around mere feet away from us. It was terrifying. It didn't even dawn on me until weeks later how bizarre it was to have a train in a ski area.

That vague thought came back to haunt me weeks later, after we'd returned home. I was watching the news and saw a report of an avalanche at St. Anton during the night. Several folks had been killed in their hotel beds. The last words of that report had been "they believe the avalanche was caused by the rumble of a train." Very sobering.

Thankfully there was no train running through Engelberg's Mt. Titlis ski resort. That was a huge relief!

Perhaps it was not in my best interest to remember these travel stories now that I think of it. And come to think of it, that had occurred on the same ski trip as our hell ride with Sparkey and Sue. Hmmmm, had I never realized that traveling with them tends to be hazardous to our health.

Remind me to tell you about their unfortunate encounter with a t-bar in Muttereralm in Innsbruck – an inconceivable challenge for them proved to be hilarious for virtually everyone skiing nearby.

I started packing for our trip but had to break to have my monthly lunch with my Marcel posse, Peg and Babs. These two, dare I say menopausal women, helped me through some of my previous murder cases like no one else. They had guts, and in true midwestern form, very little fear. Where my east coast paranoia sometimes held me back, they were always there to push me forward – for better or worse.

Babs and Peg had worked for Marcel for many years. Their protestant work ethic pulled us through many an impossible situation and helped us deliver exemplary work to the client every time. There was no job too menial or difficult for them. We all relied on them tremendously.

I walked into the restaurant and saw Babs with her tall and lanky frame and her untamed mop of a frizzy mane seated next to the much shorter Peg, whose feet I was certain were not touching the floor, with her elfish features and smooth cropped hair she spoke with 'elfin,' but commanding authority.

After a quick greeting, we chatted for a minute about their kids and Babs grandkids, but when the topic changed to my upcoming trip to Switzerland, everything shifted.

"You're going to Switzerland, Donna?" Babs asked. "I've always wanted to go there."

"You have, Babs," Peg interjected, "how did I not know that? Switzerland is definitely on my bucket list."

"Well, I," I added.

"Why don't we go now?" Peg interrupted.

"Well, we," I tried again.

"Let's do it!" Babs cut me off.

"Will you.." I tried again.

"OK, let's make sure we book on Donna's flight and get into the same hotel."

"No, hotel…"

"Yes, and we'd better hurry, it's coming up soon."

I'm pretty sure I never got a chance to utter another whole sentence before we parted ways so that my crew could book and pack. There are plenty of folks who would resent such an intrusion on their travels, but I had to admit I was thrilled at the prospect of sharing this experience with all three of my supporters, Peg, Babs and Jon. And I was sure that Dominique would get a big kick out of meeting 'the girls.' Turns out each of them might have their own connection to Switzerland and neither thought they would ever get a chance to experience it firsthand.

I'd better make sure that flat was big enough to fit all of us.

[Chapter 11]

As the plane from Chicago began to head out over the sea, Babs and Peg were chattering away like magpies. I looked over a few times and was pretty sure from the look on their faces that something unsettling had occurred to one of them.

"Jon, it's starting." I said. "They are up to something already."

Jon rolled his eyes – predictably.

Suddenly, four eyes were looking at me with intent. I unfastened my seatbelt and walked to their row, where they proceeded to fill me in.

"The guy in the seat in front of me. Don't look. I'm pretty sure he's heading to Switzerland to attend some ski races." Peg shared.

"Okayyy, so that doesn't seem terribly surprising to me." I countered.

"Right, not on its own, but he had the names of the racers and some were crossed out."

"Sooooo, could that mean he's betting on the races? I know it's not legal but…."

"Well," Peg interrupted, "he's just one of six suspicious characters we've noticed, and that's just in this section of the plane, if we start to move around the whole cabin…"

"Guys!" I whisper shouted. "We're headed off to a vacation. We are not flying to Switzerland to investigate a murder!"

"Right, we know, Donna," Babs whined. "But who knows what might happen? We have to be on top of things. We have to scope out our surroundings. It's not like we're amateurs you know."

"That is exactly what we are, Babs. We are ALL amateurs. And amateurs on our way to a fun and restful vacation trip. Try to remember, the police in Switzerland do not know us… Oh why am I trying to explain this? There is no murder to investigate! Try to keep that top of mind."

As I did the walk of shame back to my seat I could feel four eyes burning anger and frustration into my back.

"Here we go!" I said to Jon. We both rolled our eyes.

At about four hours into the flight when most everyone was asleep, Babs realized she had to use the facilities. Apparently, on the way back to her seat she decided to take a small detour behind suspected villain #1 to see what he'd been reading. Unfortunately, as she stood precariously suspended over his back the airplane experienced a slight bump. That's all that was necessary for Babs to flop over this man and knock his Kindle into the head of the man in front of him. There was a lot of yelling, the flight attendants were called and Babs was ultimately issued a warning from the plane's captain.

"But Captain," urged Peg, "My friend was just trying to get back to her seat when the plane jerked and made her fall. I hardly call that…"

Was all Peg could get out when the Captain responded "That would be the case if the man in question had not been aware of your continual watch of his every movement."

Peg started to interrupt…

"And," continued the Captain, "several folks around him had observed your odd behavior as well. That brings this incident up to borderline assault. Count your blessings we don't have the police waiting for both of you upon landing."

Great way to launch into our 'excellent adventure.'

At least I had some peace for the rest of the flight. It was just starting to dawn on me, this was going to be a long trip. If Babs and Peg saw villains every step of the way how much relaxation could I hope to achieve?

But the really sad thing is that their instincts are usually flawless. It was their actions surrounding those instincts that landed us in hot water much of the time. Once again, I had to remind myself that we were heading to an exciting vacation adventure and not rushing to the sight of a murder.

Peg and Babs didn't truly settle down until we were starting our decent into the Zurich airport. As we looked down upon the mountains and the lake we all had a bit of a religious experience gazing at the breathtaking scenery into which we were about to descend.

Once out of the airport and in the train headed for Engelberg we could all be heard to gasp out loud at the spectacular imagery all around us. We'd been so excited about seeing Dominique and the Bryners in person that we had forgotten how much of the trip would be about getting to see some of the most stunning landscape in the world, but each mile of the journey served as an unforgettable reminder.

Dominique wanted to collect us at the train station, but we insisted we'd meet her at the flat she'd arranged for us. We really put our proverbial foot down, after all she was a very busy woman. Alas, as with so many very busy women, Dominique prevailed. And there she was as we stepped out of the train, ready to haul our group on to the next phase of our adventure.

Meeting her in person for the first time was a thrill for all of us, but Dominique was focused on seeing that we were settled in and comfortable. She had made sure that the larder was stocked with all the necessities, and then some. We felt like royalty. But then, how often is even royalty pampered by a celebrity? It was so clear we were dealing with an experienced traveler who knew just how to make a journey a luxury rather than a burden.

We got the grand tour of the flat and the surrounding area and then Dominique left us to rest and get prepared to meet the Bryners at dinner that night. They had invited all of us over to a dinner at their Engelberg house and I was jumping out of my skin waiting for the time to head over there.

We had brought a few gifts for all of our new Swiss family, Dominique included. They were but a token, but we did not want to arrive empty handed. Locally U.S. made jewelry for the women, Maple syrup, California and New York wines and some U.S. ski apparel for everyone. Rest assured we knew better than to bring them chocolate or clocks.

#####

When the time finally came to head over to the Bryner house we all piled into the car. We had no trouble reaching our destination in less than 10 minutes.

After the first few minutes of greeting and gift exchanging – they had bought us quite a bit of chocolate – we immersed ourselves in getting to know one another while we also got to know chocolate that would blow your mind. Our hosts guided us through a tour of sampling starting with Felchlin and special Lindt Ragusa bars (that could not be of this earth). These were gifts like no other. In Switzerland they call it chocolate, in the U.S. we would label it something more like a religious experience.

Within a relatively short time it was as though I'd known these people all my life, and I found out later that it was the same for everyone. It truly felt like home. This was a welcoming and a sensation quite like none I'd ever experienced before.

After a brief rest from our chocolate deluge, the likes of which would make Willy Wonka gasp for air, we toured their beautiful home and were impressed by the difference in their décor and that of the flat where we stayed. While our Airbnb had a bit of Swiss flair it was very much geared toward modern, I would say even deliberately catering to American sensibilities. It was absolutely lovely, but so different from the Bryner home in that Swiss beauty and charm were exuded from every inch. While the house was in no way dated or old fashioned, it felt like a home, a Swiss home. The wood carving and the beautiful, but tasteful floral embellishments were executed to perfection. And, of course, every floor featured a magnificent cuckoo clock.

[Chapter 12]

Conversation over dinner focused mainly on skiing and ski racing. We received the schedule of where Lyra would be practicing and a few local races in which she would be competing.

Naturally, Jon wasted no time in mapping out the schedule for skiing himself. He was anxious to ski with everyone in their down time, Dominique and the Bryners. I would accompany them some of the time, definitely not on those incredibly tough Engelberg slopes, and during the rest I would accompany Peg and Babs on their sightseeing and ancestry exploration. I genuinely wanted to be able to ski in Switzerland but I also wanted to experience as much of everything as I could fit into this trip. And as you might have surmised, I really didn't want to send Peg and Babs off on their own to explore a foreign country.

That pair could get in more than enough trouble back home, and I wasn't positive we'd be able to talk our way out of a jam, or even a few small transgressions, outside of home base. In reality, some of our transgressions had not been all that small.

As we had explored our first murder together, Babs had inadvertently caused the collapse of a contractor's office building. Not a particularly large building, but still. So, in truth, not a small transgression at all. To my astonishment she had emerged from that as a hero. But how often could we count on that kind of luck?

Once all of our scheduling had been agreed upon the jet lag undeniably started to take its toll with a yawn here and a knocked over water glass there. We figured it was time to head back to the flat before we trashed the place.

The next day was amazing. I know I'm starting to sound like a broken record but there are no other words to describe what we'd been experiencing. We had a leisurely morning walking around the streets of Engelberg. Naturally, we had to stop for breakfast at The Tea Room, the scene of the first, historic meeting between Dominique and the Bryners. The place just oozed charm. Although it was not as I had imagined in my mind's eye – it was actually significantly better. Better and somewhat unexpected. The outside of the building was charming. It was light in color, and shaped to fit a uniquely wedge-shaped piece of land with Tudor timbers, a spire and delicately crafted wrought iron railings on its multiple balconies. This is the stuff of which fairytales are made.

The inside of the café with its half-round windows, simple wooden tables and chairs and lovely dark greenish/blue walls felt just like stepping into a hug.

I was worried I'd be so caught up in the charm of the place that I would neglect tasting the food. Not a problem. Once the plate of mouthwatering pastries was placed on the table my brain switched from visual to gustatory and I was off to the races with these sweet delights!

Don't worry, we didn't spend the entire day tasting. Once our appetites had been sated, we headed over to the ski area in order to watch Lyra being put through her paces.

Even though we were unable to watch her every move from our perch up on the mountain, which turned out to be the base of the ski slopes, we were able to see enough to be extremely impressed. It was a thrill for all of us riding up to the base on the gondola and walking around the frozen Trübsee. Even Babs and Peg got into the excitement and cheered along with us.

The training practice had actually begun at 8 am with some warm up runs. Then, as Dominique had enlightened us the night before, she would observe every detail and move by skiing right behind Lyra to watch her every turn. Then they would proceed to the set up course, which we would not be able to see without being on skis, where they would focus on speed and how slight changes in her movement would enable her to ski faster – which is obviously the end goal.

We had arrived about mid-morning when they were moving into more "free" skiing on the slopes and focusing on one or two technical steps that they had analyzed earlier that morning. We were able to view most of these exercises. I realized that Dominique has quite a sense of humor when she deliberately slowed her skiing down to a snail's pace expecting Lyra to follow suit. It was a little like watching a circus act and you could see that Lyra struggled at first because going exceptionally slow requires a whole different set of balance skills and it also fails to hide any imperfections that are easier to camouflage with speed.

Once the training practice was finished we were able to treat the group to a late lunch slopeside to share our excitement with the entire crew. As charming as the rustic wood restaurant appeared and as scrumptious as the food proved to be, not to mention the stupendous views out the window, our attention was on Lyra and her exchange with Dominique.

Although we understood that Dominique would never critique Lyra's execution in front of our group, Lyra, as is true of most serious athletes, spent part of the time critiquing her own performance and looking to Dominique for advice. And true to form, if a question was asked of her, Dominique would provide a straightforward response, i.e. she wasn't about to soft soap anything.

At first I felt a bit uncomfortable not wanting to see Lyra at a vulnerable time, but I should have known better. Lyra had no such qualms, she wanted to spend her time with Dominique in the most productive way possible and we had a front row seat in watching their exchange. It was fascinating.

Initially, Lyra complained about her backward position on the skis and that she tried to push her knees forward just like the coaches always told her.

Dominique asked, "What were your arms and hands doing when you felt this backward position on the skis."

"I'm talking about my leg position," Lyra insisted, "nothing to do with my arms."

"I'm sorry but it has everything to do with your arms," replied

Dominique, "can you even recall where your arms were, can you show me the position?" Dominique asked.

Lyra made some general movement and then confessed she has no idea about where her arms are during her turns. Dominique told her to try to watch her arm movement during the next few runs.

"Instead of trying harder to push your knees forward, focus on your arms. Do the movements your feet should do and the forward movement your knees should do with your arms and hands. The legs will follow automatically."

It was as though they were in their own little world and although I could kind of follow their dialogue they spoke as though no one else could hear them. It was an intensity of communication that you don't often see or hear.

The next day my posse and I figured on hitting some of the sights. We had planned on renting a car but Dominique would not hear of it. By this time we had learned not to argue with Dominique when her mind was made up. She was already doing so much for us, but we would just add the car to that list. At any rate, today's sightseeing would be easily accessible by public transport or even by foot.

Our first stop was Talmuseum Engelberg and when finished, we would be able to just walk around the corner to the Benedictine Church and monastery.

The Talmuseum was such a treat. Located in an historical farmhouse and featuring traditional Swiss furnishings, this combined with the lovely historical artifacts was my favorite kind of Museum. You could virtually see life in the late 18th century. The newer part of the museum also exhibited some extremely clever design features. I could have stayed there for days, especially since they have a 5-year long exhibition on all the Olympic medal winners. Remarkably, Engelberg is the town with the most Olympic medals (15) and the medals are on display. Naturally Dominique and her sister, Michelle are featured prominently. It's not like I didn't know what they've achieved, but it was so impressive to see it featured in a legendary museum.

The Monastery and Church were every bit as impactful. The grace and beauty of these edifices juxtaposed against the difficulty of life back then left an imposing impression on the visitor. Suffice it to say we had an exceptional day.

While we were immersing ourselves in the history and culture of this quiet little area of Switzerland, we couldn't help but notice the cleanliness of everything, everywhere. Coming from the U.S. where public service ad campaigns have been running for years to remind us to "Keep America Beautiful" and clean, we were still falling considerably short of what the Swiss had accomplished from what we were able to observe.

Meanwhile, in another part of Engelberg, Jon was getting the lowdown from Dominique on where he should plan to ski. In her usual thorough way, she was filling him in on every ski area within a fairly wide range. Likewise Jon, in his own thorough way was grilling Dominique for every last detail about each area. After about an hour of sharing details and ski stories Jon noticed that Dominique had started to look very thoughtful.

"What are you thinking about, Dominique?"

She smiled, took a breath and shared a favorite childhood memory.

"When I was a kid I always went to ski vacation for a week with my grandparents. This is rather funny thinking that I grew up in a ski area, but my granddad (Opa) was in love with Andermatt, especially the skiing mountain Gemsstock. He spent many many skiing days on that hill. But, of course, my teammates would make fun of me going skiing with my grandparents once I was 12 and later. I can promise you though that those skiing days were super tough. Always starting with the first gondola and ending with the last. Counting, of course, the number of glacier passages, one of the hardest slopes in Andermatt, and not really seeing much of a restaurant from the inside no matter the weather…."

That was when Jon truly understood what a special place Andermatt must be for Dominique.

[Chapter 13]

Back in our flat that night, Babs, Peg and I filled Jon in on our day of exploration. He listened politely and asked a lot of questions. When he filled us in on his conversation with Dominique there was a tiny glisten in his eye. It wasn't difficult to see that Dominique's reminiscence about her days of skiing with her grandfather had touched him deeply.

As a teen Jon had worked for his grandfather's construction company during summers. Those were some of the most physically exacting days of his life, but they meant more to him than anything. The bond he formed with his grandfather was a major factor throughout his life. He could absolutely relate to Dominique's sentiments.

We soon got busy with scheduling for the next few days. It was this kind of coordination that made such a multifaceted trip run smoothly. Once everything was laid out based on the available information, we knew that the next day would be our first chance to see Lyra in an actual race. It would be held in the Engelberg ski area on slope Erika and would be a local/regional event, but these were just the kinds of experience she needed in order to move her career on to the next level.

#####

The next morning we arrived at the bottom Station of Titlis with a few minutes to spare and the Bryners had not yet made their appearance.

Little did I know, the only way to view this race would be to navigate a somewhat tricky slope – on skis. The mountain staff kindly pointed out the "easier" way – easier to them – not so easy to some of the rest of us. I'm thinking Dominique kept that to herself for a very good reason!

But, what Dominique did not know, was that neither Babs nor Peg had ever been on skis before. What surely presented a daunting challenge for me would be an impossibility for them. Whose idea had it been to drag them along this morning? Oh yeah, that would be me.

As they were fitted with their gear, the mountain staff were immediately able to assess our challenge. Peg and Babs were equipped, not only with their rental skiing gear, but each with an individual mountain guide to practically carry them down the slope to a spot near the Stand. I was left to fend for myself with a little help and encouragement from Jon and Dominique.

With Dominique's guidance and a great deal of help from the mountain staff, we all arrived at the area known as The Stand – the meeting point on the mountain - unscathed. Now that we had overcome this initial hurdle, I could see the concerned look on Dominique's face. Where were the Bryners? But, being the trooper she was, she kept it light.

"You know, Donna," Dominique started, "This may be the first time I am seeing you dressed in clothing that is not all black."

This was an understatement considering my Italian ski jacket was a vibrant orangey-red. This was another brilliantly sunny day in the Swiss mountains and the sun bounced off the metallic colors in a blinding display. Every movement I made was a shooting starburst assaulting the eyes of everyone around me. Don't judge me – it was marked down to an insanely low price and it's Italian! – I had no choice!

"I always forget about the effect of the "all black" wardrobe on non-advertising folks. You know, Dominique, I worked in the Northeast in the days when, if you showed up for a meeting anywhere near NYC wearing any color but black you stood out like a wedding cake in a weight loss clinic. I just got in that habit of all black all the time and never really felt comfortable in any other color. Occasionally now, in the summer, I will wear either a top or bottom in another color – but never the entire ensemble, as evidenced by my black ski pants!"

"Well, I guess we missed that trend here in Europe, although I do see a lot of black outfits on my lecture tour."

Our little wardrobe chat acted as a distraction, helping me catch my breath, and keeping us all from worrying for just a moment as the time for the race grew closer and The Bryners were still not here. This did not bode well.

Just as I was about to make a comment four of the Bryner's skied up to us with apologies for cutting it so close.

"Nevermind that," said Dominique, "Is Lyra all set with her gear?

"She's got everything except her skis, she's heading over to get them from the racer's ski rack in the basement of that building." Will offered, pointing to the only building in the area.

"Ski over to pick your viewing spot while I go to meet Lyra for warm up and race inspection. It will still be a few minutes before any racing begins," as Dominique was saying this she was shooing us all to ski in the direction of the best viewing area. We knew that we would not see Lyra again until she was racing down the slope and the air was virtually buzzing with excitement.

Within moments we heard a huge crash causing all of us to jump. As we looked toward Dominique for reassurance we saw her kick off her skis and run hell bent for leather, in the direction of the building.

Once realization hit us we began to follow behind her knowing full well we would not be able to keep up either on skis or on foot. We all abandoned our skis and ran as fast as our ski boots would allow.

We watched as Dominique entered the building just as two of the mountain staffers came out and began instructing everyone else to remain outside. We asked some lift operators to explain but they were vague in their response while looking extremely unnerved. That did not help to calm us down.

After a few moments Dominique reappeared. The look on her face did not assuage our concern.

"What happened," she began "is the massive metal and wood ski rack, inside the building, that holds all the racing skis has collapsed leaving a pile of broken metal, wood and skis."

"But Lyra was just heading in there to get her skis," Greta cried, "did you see her?"

"I did not see Lyra but I am certain we will find her," Dominique tried to reassure us all. But her face belied her concern. "I looked around as much as I was able, but the security guards ushered me away from the building as the dust and debris was still rising from the pile of rubble. At least they know to watch for her."

I stole a quick glance at Babs and got a glare and a snarl in return. I knew she couldn't have done it – she was right with me the whole time, but with her history…

We were all feeling somewhat frantic, but there was little we could do but wait. The Bryner kids and Babs and Peg shouted their intent to scour the area for any signs of Lyra while Will tried his best to comfort Greta as well as himself. No one spoke. There was really nothing to say.

After about 20 minutes some members of the rescue squad emerged from the building.

"Can you tell if there are any injuries?" asked Dominique.

"We are not yet able to see everything that has been buried under all the debris, but we do believe it is possible that one or two people may have been trapped when the rack fell over. There are indications that there is some clothing in the rubble and it appears as though at least one of the injured is a staffer since some of the shredded clothing looks very much like our mountain ski jackets."

That's when Greta really started to lose it.

"Oh my god, Will, what if our precious girl is in there? I want to go in and yell for her, I can't wait here anymore, I have to do something."

It was heartbreaking to see the anguish on these poor parents. How could something like this possibly happen? We knew the last thing the rescue folks would allow was a desperate and nearly hysterical Mother under foot as they tried to work their fastest and safest to find any casualties.

As more workers moved among the crowd we realized they had clearly been trained to withhold any information until the sum total of the ramifications had been discovered, but their faces had begun to look more grave than ever.

Babs had returned with no luck in finding Lyra. She made a move to head inside the building. I body checked her remembering that she alone had brought down a whole building in the past. We did not need that right now.

The waiting was agony. And if I felt this bad I could only imagine how Will and Greta must feel. What a nightmare. At some point it dawned on me that the waiting and not knowing might just be the best we'd feel if, god forbid, anything had happened to Lyra. I had to force my brain to shut down. This kind of thinking was only making things worse.

The whole staff at the mountain had been put to work in jobs that didn't exist previously, but had become crucial in this emergency. Several staffers were charged with walking the grounds and finding all of the racers and their guests. They were busily making the rounds with their ipads poised to collect the crucial data.

We grabbed one of the women and asked if she'd seen Lyra.

"I have not spoken to anyone named Lyra."

We immediately deflated.

"But," she continued, "I think a liftie may have spoken to a young woman named Lyra when I was on the other side of the building."

With our hope restored we all ran around the building. When we got there the crowd was much bigger and noisier. We frantically searched the faces for Lyra and asked every third or fourth person. Just as we were about ready to give up hope we spied a young woman sitting on a bench about 30 feet from the building, and miraculously it was Lyra!

We didn't know what to do first. We laughed, we cried a little, we hugged everyone in sight – even complete strangers. It was the most amazing relief. And poor Lyra was practically being smothered by our group as well as the onlookers who came to realize what we had feared.

As the ruckus began to calm down and the onlookers moved on to watch the action that was still unfolding we noticed that Lyra looked crestfallen. Dominique managed to recover herself sooner than the rest of us and she asked Lyra:

"Why are you looking so sad, Lyra, "what is worrying you."

"I was about to get my skis. They were the closest ones to the door. As I headed down the stairs, before reaching the door to the ski storage room, I heard a strange rumbling sound. It scared me so much that I just ran upstairs and out of the building."

We all started talking at once.

"Yes, thank the good lord…"

"That was the smartest thing you could have done…"

"Thank goodness you were able to think so quickly…"

"So Lyra," continued Dominique, "you acted fast and saved yourself from severe injury or even death, why are you now looking so defeated."

"Because I did not think fast enough to take my skis and I am sure they have been crushed along with everything else."

That comment was the final straw that broke through all the tension. We laughed and hugged and applauded Lyra for being such a clever girl. Lyra did not share in our jubilation. Apparently, only Dominique could fully understand what, to Lyra, was beyond tragedy.

"You know, Lyra, I have had many pairs of skis in my career and I do understand the attachment. But I have to say that as well as I may have skied over the years, I never started to win until a top athlete willed me her skis. I do understand your melancholy but that pair of skis was most certainly not going to be the pair that enables you to win the important ski races. There will be other pairs far more important to you in your life"

"Really? You raced with somebody else's old brokendown skis?"

"Well, you must remember that racing skis are treated with kid gloves – literally. It would be difficult to find a pair of racing skis that are "broken down" unless they were in an accident. But to answer your question, yes, racing skis used by top athletes are often the best skis you can hope to get, and they are indisputably the fastest based on how they've been used and cared for. Being willed a pair of these skis is one of the greatest honors in the industry."

At that, Lyra perked up quite a bit and we decided that since the race had been called off for that day, we would all head out and take the long journey, via gondola, to our cars in order to grab some lunch at Restaurant Bierlialp.

As we started to walk toward the car we saw the ambulance start to drive slowly away. Dominique ran over to the group of officials watching the ambulance depart in the hope of finding that it left because it was unnecessary. We just stood anxiously waiting for her return as two uniformed polizei walked toward us.

"Is this the young woman who escaped the building just moments before the crash? We will need to ask her a few questions before allowing her to exit the mountain.

"Now let us begin with the reason you were entering the building."

It was clear from their questions that the polizei were trying to determine what role, if any, Lyra had in the collapse of the ski rack. We were easily able to assure them that, based on the fact that she had never been alone in the hours prior to the incident, she was not in any way responsible.

"Can you then explain why you decided to run from the building before completing the task of retrieving your skis?"

Once Lyra explained about the noise that she'd heard, the polizei were frantically noting every word. They questioned her, at length, about the exact sounds and their precise volume. It was clear that, at this point in the investigation, they were obsessively obtaining any nugget of information that could help them determine exactly what had occurred.

Upon Dominique's return to the group we learned that sadly, the news she'd acquired was not as hoped.

"I am sad to say that this incident was not without tragedy. It appears as though one person was fatally injured. Although they have not yet made a positive identification, it is rumored that it is the body of a businessman from the U.S. This determination was made somewhat from his mode of dress – although that was a bit confusing, plus the origin of the clothing and a few notes in his pocket. The early responders were thrown by the fact that there was a mountain staff jacket right there – which is odd since there was only the one body meaning, thankfully, not also a tragedy for one of our staff members. They hope to recover the victim's wallet and phone, although as yet they have had no luck."

Immediately upon hearing Dominique's news, the polizei ran over to the gathered officials. Clearly, this was the first they were hearing the news of the tragedy and the focus of the investigation would soon be changing dramatically.

After all the ups and downs of fearing for Lyra, finding Lyra, this tragic news shocked the rest of the energy out of all of us. We were speechless for the first time. Lyra and her siblings cried at the thought of Lyra's close call. And her parents were too stunned to react at all.

Babs and Peg took control in their usual manner.

"Come on," said Peg, "let's all get to that lovely restaurant. We'll get a shot of whiskey with honey for the grownups and a pastry for the kids. A little sugar will do us all some good."

With that we slowly made our way to the parking lot and then on to Restaurant Bierlialp. Once there, the beautifully carved wood – even the ceiling featured wood turned artwork - began to ease our tension. It was a cozy and inviting place and we ate a delicious yet somber lunch while we continued to reset our nervous systems. Much to our surprise, our meal was an expertly prepared Italian treat. When in the German speaking areas of Switzerland it is easy to forget that almost 10% of the population is Italian, and clearly they take their cuisine as seriously as do their counterparts in Italy.

I made up my mind that we would return to Restaurant Bierlialp again before going home. I wanted to experience this exceptional cuisine once more and without the haze of shock that enveloped us all.

[Chapter 14]

After lunch, Dominique was anxious to check on any further information that had been gleaned from examination of the ski area. It was essential that she learn what area or areas were considered an accident or a crime scene as well as how likely it was that the entire mountain would be closed and, if possible, for how long. She was also concerned about the damage to the racing skis. So many athletes would be impacted by this one destructive and ultimately tragic event.

With Dominique otherwise engaged, and the Bryner family heading home to regroup, the rest of us decided to stroll around the streets of Engelberg. We were determined not to miss even a small amount of time when we could be experiencing this magical place, but in truth, we were not in the mood to attack our bucket list with all that much gusto.

Later that evening, Dominique stopped by our flat to fill us in on what she'd learned. At first she had learned very little other than that the mountain would operate as usual, but the portion of the building housing the large racing ski rack would be closed for further investigation. She was also told that none of the skis on the rack appeared to be salvageable, and although none of the skiers planning on participating in the day's races were considered top athletes, she knew that this would be a discouraging blow to all of them.

As luck would have it, one of the officers assigned to guard the building was a fellow ski racer of Dominique's back in the early days. So, Officer Bachmann, or Hermann as Dominique knew him, was more willing to share some of the key details with his former racing companion. This was a huge plus, although what he did share made it clear that not much had, as yet, been ascertained.

In an effort to get a clear picture of precisely what had occurred the police had decided to leave the scene untouched aside from extricating the sole victim.

Officer Bachmann, or Hermann, shared that they were puzzled on several key issues. What was a U.S. businessman doing lurking near a racing ski rack in Switzerland? What had caused an extremely sturdy ski rack to suddenly crash forward? They found extraneous material that would possibly suggest some sort of trip wire, but who wanted to trip someone, presumably a racer, and who did they want to trip? With all of these questions remaining they were not inclined to move anything at the scene.

Where they had made progress was in a list of potential intended victims and perpetrators. At the top of the list of intended victims was Lyra and the deceased U.S. businessman because of their proximity to the scene at the time of the accident. There were a few more stragglers, workers inside the building and possibly even other racers and non-racing skiers who had wandered into an area where they should not have been.

As far as the list of possible perpetrators went, the deceased topped that list, but without knowledge of his exact identify and any motive, things were at somewhat of a standstill. There were others on that list, but luckily Lyra was quickly eliminated based on the timing of when she entered the building. Her whole family's recorded arrival time provided Lyra with a strong alibi. There was no way she would have had a chance of sabotaging the ski rack.

Police had virtually eliminated the possibility that this could have been an accident. The extraneous odds and ends found, although still a mystery, were far too much of a coincidence to suggest a mere misfortune. However, their investigation would pursue all avenues until there was more certainty.

At this time, it seemed their mindset was fixated on the fact that the deceased had been the intended victim, but there was no indication of who would want to harm or kill him and certainly nothing to suggest they would want to kill him near the ski rack – except for the fact that he was found dead there. They could find no other connection to skiing or racing.

It occurred to me that if we'd been in Omaha, I would already have started my investigation. While I could feel the spark of temptation I was smart enough to realize that language and cultural differences would make investigating this incident much more difficult than those I'd investigated with my associates in the states. And, as yet, we didn't know that this was a murder. But I could feel that old tingling sensation telling me that this most certainly was a murder.

Once Dominique had filled us in on her intel I knew precisely what we had to do.

"Jon, we have to call Tom."

"Tom?"

"Tom Royce. He will be able to examine the pile of wood and metal and extraneous odd objects and piece together the exact chain of events."

"You're right!"

Dominique looked at us curiously so I explained.

"Tom has a business that can build and/or refurbish almost anything with wood or metal. The police in Iowa and Nebraska often consult him when there is a suspicious occurrence involving either material. He has been responsible for helping to solve any number of mysteries and getting him involved here will save on time and accuracy."

"Then let's contact him immediately," Dominique urged.

Jon was already making the call.

While Tom and Jon were on the phone, they were also looking up flight availabilities and then booking a flight. Tom would join us the day after tomorrow and help us get to the bottom of the mystery.

Once we had Tom's details locked and loaded, Dominique suggested that we have one of the police officers with whom Tom had consulted give the Swiss Police a call to alleviate any concerns about his status as an expert consultant. Jon jumped on that as well and was pleasantly surprised at how eager the Swiss police were to get Tom's insights into precisely what had occurred. He had assumed he'd have to do some persuading, but as exacting as the Swiss can be, they do not mince words when it comes to getting the right expert into the right situation. Egos do not factor into their calculations, they want to get it right, and fast.

Dominique turned to me and with that slightly eerie ability she had to read my mind, she said:

"So, Donna, the fact that you are from the U.S., as is the deceased, should prove helpful to our investigation."

"Our investigation?"

"Of course, with our combined backgrounds, and especially with your impressive history as a detective, we are the perfect team to solve this mystery."

"Dominique." I smiled, "I couldn't agree with you more."

[Chapter 15]

The next day was perfect for a ski trip to Andermatt. Lyra would still be able to get in some quality practice and we would all get a chance to take a breath and escape the drama and lingering sadness and confusion that sat heavily on each of us from the previous day's occurrences.

I used that skiing time to organize my thoughts. I mentally prepared a list of questions for Tom, another list for Dominique to ask her cop friend, although I'm sure Dominique had her own list of questions for each. We had agreed to each formulate our path forward and meet after dinner to compare notes and consolidate our thinking. That would keep us from stepping on each other's toes. There would be times in this investigation when we would divide and conquer and other times when it would be imperative that we work side by side.

I also planned on filling Dominique in on the unorthodox help I'd always received from my posse, Babs and Peg. The hope was that it would enable her to know when to bring them along, but also to be on guard for falling buildings, at least whenever Babs was near.

By lunchtime at the lodge both Dominique and I had already planned our strategies and the resulting questions. We compared notes over a lovely soup/stew concoction and found that, to our amazement, many of our thoughts were identical. It made me wish that Dominique had been there for the three prior murders I'd been given credit for solving. Perhaps if she had, things would not have gotten to such a scary point. Oh well, best not to speculate about past murders. Clearly, we were ready to get to work on this one.

The most important part of our strategic approach was that it was ready to implement immediately. We would not have to wait until tomorrow since we were both aware that time was of the essence and that murders are most easily solved within the first few days.

We finished our lunch by creating a timeline for the next two or three moves and assigning the person or persons to handle each task. There was no point in planning more than a day or two ahead since we knew full well that each step could completely alter all following steps.

"You know it didn't occur to me that one very frustrating part of investigating a murder would be the inability to plan very far ahead. When I'm racing, I am able to plan things out for weeks or even months. That does not mean certain outcomes won't alter my plans, but it rarely happens to this extent, when you are sure you have found the murderer – if there even is a murderer in this case, and the next day you are convinced it is someone quite different." Dominique commented.

"Excellent observation, Dominique, I find that is why I so often feel like a complete moron when I get involved in these investigations, I feel as though I'm all over the place. I am used to planning things out, but when murder is involved being able to pivot becomes the most important attribute. And when one finds oneself in mortal danger that ability to pivot can quite literally make all the difference in staying alive."

True to our plan, by mid-afternoon we proceeded to implement our strategy. First on the list was to have Dominique talk to her officer friend again. Any information he felt comfortable sharing with his good friend would save us a ton of time and aggravation. We knew he would still be hanging around the scene as the daily operations of the ski area could potentially jeopardize the ski rack/murder weapon and therefore, the scene itself.

While Dominique began her in-depth inquiry with Officer Bachmann, Jon and I drove to the train station to pick up Tom. We assumed he'd want to drop in to our flat to freshen up and drop off his stuff. We should have known better. Tom had already arranged to meet the officer responsible for crime scene forensics at the sight. He wasn't about to waste a second to allow the scene to deteriorate any further.

"The more the materials shift the more difficult it will be to pinpoint exactly what transpired," Tom said, "I didn't fly all this way to let that happen."

"Tom, we've got your back. Whatever you need. Trust me, we'll make sure nothing gets in the way of your mission," Jon responded.

As we drove back to Titlis we did our best to encourage Tom to hang around for a bit even after he'd reached his conclusions about the incident. I think we had him at world class beer and the description of our unearthly chocolate indoctrination didn't hurt either.

#####

While Jon and Tom proceeded to the accident site, Dominique and I headed upstairs in the lodge to try and chat with as many of the staff as we were able. It hadn't occurred to us, but the sheer violence of the incident had been bottled up inside of these poor folks. They could not talk enough about everything and anything. That made our interviews much easier – we didn't have to force anyone to talk – and that would also make things much more difficult – we learned every detail about every minor thing from who turned the lights on in what room to who got a band aid for the little boy who skinned his knee. Too much information? Yes. But in this sort of investigation there is no detail too small – you never know what choice nugget might be buried in the most menial of stories shared. That's what the detectives in Omaha taught me and it really helped deal with the boredom of this avalanche of information. Under the circumstances, avalanche may have been a poor choice of words.

As gentle as we tried to be, it was clear that these folks were way too traumatized for us to get much of anything useful out of them. We tried our best to observe their body language thinking this would help us figure out who best to target for a later interview. Out of about 30 staffers, there were nearly 10 who exhibited enough oddities to capture our attention.

An hour and a half later, Dominique nodded to me. We would be back to interview everyone, but we had a short list of folks who would be getting specific questions from us. And, if nothing else, we had primed all of them to begin searching their minds for anything unusual they had observed before, during and after the incident had occurred.

[Chapter 16]

That night over dinner at our flat – Jon and Tom volunteered to barbecue ribs for everyone – we discussed our progress with the case. It was truly amazing to me how much ground we'd managed to cover in such a short time.

Tom had set up a workstation to test various parts from the materials that crashed at the scene. I had a strong feeling that he already knew exactly what happened, but true to form he was going to test out every part of his theory to ensure the highest level of accuracy.

Dominique appeared to have made the most progress in talking to her friend, Hermann. It seems the Polizei had already verified that the victim was an American. They located his hotel and were able to find all of his identification, including his passport. They were still unsure as to why this American had chosen to visit a ski area with no ski equipment or clothing except a mountain staff ski jacket that was not his. Actually, the Engelberg mountain is often the host of visitors who are not prepared to ski so this is not all that unusual until you combine it with the fact that he carried no identification and a "borrowed" mountain jacket. There was something very "off" about this particular visitor.

Further investigation chronicled our victim as a relatively shiftless individual. Apparently, he was from a rural area of Pennsylvania, but had moved around as his nefarious activities had caught up with him in each place he had lived. His name was Beauford "Beau" Jones. Jones had done some time in the State Correctional Institution in Albion, PA.

As I listened to Dominique's recant of Officer Hermann's findings, something about Beau's Pennsylvania roots pushed at the corners of my mind. What was it about his being located in Pennsylvania that was niggling at me? Ahhh, forget it. The more I pushed myself the more I knew it would come to me in its own time, and not one minute sooner. I would have to be patient, and that was decidedly not my best attribute!

But why had this 'ne'er-do-well' foreigner been found dead in a tragic equipment failure, a possible accident, in a Swiss ski area? Was it just that the black cloud over his head in the U.S. had followed him to Switzerland and multiplied greatly upon touchdown? Was he an intended murder victim? Who here knew him and would want to kill him? Or was he, perhaps, a bungling failure of a murderer himself? And, if so, who was his intended victim? There were still way too many questions needing answers.

When we started to examine all of Beau's history, the information that Hermann had discovered so far, a pattern of failure began to emerge. It seemed as though everything Mr. Jones had attempted had stupendously dissolved into unmitigated failure. This guy was the dictionary definition of Sad Sack.

Wisely, Hermann had advised Dominique that his research into Jones' background had barely scratched the surface. It seemed as though our answers were more likely to emerge from the U.S. than from right here where the incident had occurred. Most unusual.

For a few moments we all sat, each lost in our thoughts, eating our barbeque.

"Pennsylvania," Will said quietly, "I did some training there."

Why was that word, Pennsylvania, pinging harder and harder against my brain? And still, it would not come to me.

#####

The next day Tom was hard at his make-shift workshop. Jon was by his side to lend a helping hand. I was flitting about feeling somewhat useless and trying not to bug Tom for answers before he felt ready.

Dominique had a nearly full day working with Lyra, and Babs and Peg had decided to explore their own "Swiss Connections."

I was reluctant to pursue the investigation much further without Dominique's guidance. The last thing I wanted to do was upset or anger staffers, skiers and especially not the Polizei, but I was fully charged and ready for action!

As I roamed around the ski area in search of a task that would not end up causing more harm than good I ran into Dominique's friend, Officer Bachmann.

"Ahh, Frau Leigh, I see you are on your own today. Have your friends all deserted you?" he asked with a chuckle.

"It appears so, Officer Bachmann. I am feeling kind of useless right about now, just hoping to stay out of trouble."

"Well, let me share a bit of information that should help to change your outlook."

I perked up immediately.

"It seems that Herr Jones had managed to accumulate an enormous number of enemies in his short time on earth. Our informants tell us that there were any number of people who would have paid good money to see him to his grave."

That elevated my spirits even more! And he continued...

"I have learned that there is a town in Pennsylvania that is labeled 'The Switzerland of America' and it boasts the very unusual name of 'Jim Thorpe.'"

"Jim Thorpe, Pennsylvania?" I asked skeptically.

"That's correct, Frau Leigh. Jim Thorpe, Pennsylvania."

Well, I'll be damned.

"And furthermore, Jim Thorpe is where Herr Jones spent a great deal of his time, defrauding the good folks of Swiss heritage residing there. So, there are a great number of folks with Swiss ancestry who would happily attend the funeral of Beauford Jones. The connection is there."

"That's great! Oh, but that's awful. We just widened the suspect pool from a handful of skiers and resort staff to anyone in Switzerland with a Swiss connection, native or tourist," I lamented.

"Frau Leigh, we will take our investigation one step at a time and follow the thread that leads us to our answers. We do not despair at a widened suspect pool – it merely means that our journey to the truth is progressing."

Wow, these Swiss police were deep thinkers. I was seriously impressed. But I was also feeling that niggling feeling about Pennsylvania. What could that possibly mean; would it shed any light on this investigation? And when would I remember what it was?

When Dominique had finished her session with Lyra, she decided to stop off at the flat to see if anyone else had made it back. After a quick knock she determined that no one had returned yet, so she started to head out again. That's when she ran into Babs and Peg all excited from their 'Swiss connection' quest.

Seeing them gave Dominique an idea. She had been thinking about doing some more due diligence at the Talstation (or lodge in U.S. vernacular) and its surroundings with a very specific purpose. It had occurred to her that no one interviewed had professed to setting eyes on the murder victim prior to finding him dead. She felt the need to explore this oddity further, and felt Babs and Peg would be the perfect team to accompany her in her mission given their successful sleuthing in the U.S.

Once apprised of her objective, Babs and Peg were ready and willing. The three hopped into Dominique's car and headed back to Titlis ski area. The game plan, as outlined by Dominique, was to question everyone they saw on that one specific detail – had they seen this individual moving about the Station or its surrounding area? Dominique had secured a copy of the victim's photo during one of her conversations with her friend, Hermann, still Officer Bachmann to us, for help with identification.

The three worked diligently trying to find even one individual who had seen the victim while still alive. The more folks they interviewed the more perplexed they became. How was it possible for someone who stood out like a sore thumb to elude attention from anyone at all? The question also arose that, if this man had successfully avoided being seen by literally everyone, was that something he'd done deliberately? If so, that would certainly make it seem as though he was not only the victim, but also the murderer. Why else would he have worked so hard to keep himself out of sight of everyone? And, if he was hiding from an assailant, why hide in a ski area with no evidence of being a skier?

One thing we felt sure of, no one would fly to a foreign country and select an environment even more foreign to them, and in which they stood no chance of blending in, to commit suicide. So, we felt justified in ruling that out altogether.

Dominique felt there was one last place to check. At the side of the après ski chalet, at the bottom Station, that was the most obscure, with no views of either the parking lot or the mountain, there was an attic storage room. Staffers were in and out of this room on a regular basis looking for anything from foodservice utensils to cleaning products and even lift ticket paraphernalia and bar equipment. She believed that if the three waited around the storeroom for an hour or so they would manage to interview the folks who frequented that area. If the victim had been hiding in that storeroom, it was these staffers who would likely have noticed something unusual or out-of-place.

As they waited Babs and Peg regaled Dominique with stories of our prior sleuthing. Time went by quickly as Dominique laughed at the various challenges we had faced. Babs being Babs both talked and walked around inside the storage room inspecting every inch and every box stored.

At one point, the 4 pm bartender getting ready for his shift, stopped by for a case of soda. The three immediately began to quiz him as to whether or not he'd seen Beau Jones. Although he denied actually having seen the man, he did recall that some of the boxes that had been stacked in the corner for years had been moved to another section of the room. It hadn't registered with him until Peg asked if he'd noticed anything unusual.

As far as Dominique and her crew were concerned, they had finally found evidence that Beau had not only been in the lodge prior to his last and final visit under the wreckage of the ski rack, but he had been intent on hiding. That was a huge finding. Either Beau had been hiding from a potential murderer who was out to get him or Beau had been a potential murderer out to get someone else. But once again, who?

The team was satisfied they had garnered the information they'd set out to get and were preparing to head out. True to form, Babs decided she'd help the bartender locate and move everything he needed even though he assured her he was more than capable of handling the task on his own.

"No need to worry, young man," Babs assured him, "I know what a pain this kind of stuff can be and I'm happy to help in any way you need."

As she was reassuring the bartender, Babs noticed he was about to step on an unstable looking floorboard. Realizing that she would not be able to explain her concerns in time she did what she thought would fix everything, she yanked on the board to right it just as the bartender was stepping down.

Dominique and Peg watched in horror as the bartender stepped down on air. His leg went right through the floor landing him hard on his butt with his other leg in an unlikely position.

"Oh god," said Peg, "here we go."

"But I, you know I," Babs sputtered.

"So, this is what Donna was talking about." Dominique lost no time in checking on the bartender's injuries. Before she had made a complete assessment, three other staffers came flying up the stairs hoping to find the owner of the leg that was now hanging down over the kitchen prep area.

With everyone working together they managed to free up the bartender's leg, which seemed to be fine. His other leg, however, had suffered some injury when abruptly slammed into the floor. The hope was that it was nothing more than a sprain, but it was necessary to try and locate the staffers trained in first aid in order to determine the necessary steps.

#####

Once back at the flat, Dominique shared their findings with Jon, Tom and me. But first, she entertained them with the soon to be legendary story of Babs, the bartender and his dangling leg.

After hearing all about the storeroom and the bartender's observations everyone had to agree that Beau had been hiding there for some reason – and that fact alone indicated that this incident was far more nefarious than a simple but tragic accident. It would be especially interesting to hear of Tom's findings. Should he find evidence of foul play it would leave no doubt whatsoever that this was indeed a murder – or an attempted murder gone wrong.

After that heavy realization, talk of Babs and her latest faux pas helped to lighten up everyone's mood. Babs continued to sputter her justification to no avail.

"Honey," I stopped her, "don't even bother, your reputation precedes you."

"You know," Dominique observed, "now I really feel as though I am officially part of the team!"

Babs beamed. I just rolled my eyes.

[Chapter 17]

First thing this morning, Tom announced he was meeting with the polizei to share his findings. He suggested we meet for lunch so he could fill us all in afterward.

No one wanted to venture too far afield. We were all anxious to hear what Tom had to say. Even Will and Greta had popped over in hopes of hearing that the whole thing could be ruled an unfortunate accident and life could start to get back to normal. They chose to keep the children away in the event that their hopes were dashed and this tragic occurrence proved to be something far more sinister.

We decided the best use of our time would be to regroup and realign our action steps while awaiting Tom's return. It appeared as though a great deal understandably revolved around our victim, Beau. In a nutshell, we decided to double down on our efforts to learn about Beau and his background. To date, all we really knew was that he was a great deal less than an upstanding citizen. In fact, by all accounts, so far, he was basically the antithesis of an upstanding citizen – and he wasn't even very good at that.

After kicking things around for a bit longer, we started to prepare lunch in honor of Tom's return. Our luncheon fare consisted of various sliced meats, cheeses, potatoes and bread. I knew this would appeal to Tom and his love of potatoes. Greta suggested we include a cream sauce for the sliced meat – which would be good for the others but poison for me with my lactose intolerance – hence the cream sauce with Greta's family recipe was served on the side.

Over lunch Tom filled us in on his investigation. He was able to determine that the ski rack had been deliberately sabotaged. And while the polizei had assumed as much, Tom was able to pinpoint with great accuracy, precisely what had been tampered with.

"First and foremost, the ski rack had been built with far more support than was necessary. It was clear that the folks operating the lodge understood the importance of overcompensating for the structure of a rack of this immense size not to mention importance. And, if you're thinking that time was the enemy here you would be mistaken. The rack had been built less than three years earlier. There's no way time would have caused this kind of failure with the quality of materials used and the age of the rack. Whoever tampered with this ski rack knew what they were doing and did so deliberately."

This last statement of Tom's hit us all like a gut punch. We had known all along that this was a possibility, even a probability, but to hear it confirmed struck terror in all of our hearts. Who would want to do this? Who were they trying to hurt? And why? Tom continued.

"The rack itself was built with two by sixes of Swiss Larch, a very dense timber recognizable by its light-red decorative color and most frequently used in outdoor construction. It was then reinforced with a corresponding steel frame that could have withstood a tornado and an earthquake together. The weakest part of the entire structure was the fact that it was raised up by five-inch wooden legs. That seemed unusual to me until one of the local carpenters explained that, on occasion, when there is a lot of snow and a sudden melt, there can be water rushing through the first floor and into the lower floor of the lodge. And while that doesn't happen very often, the carpenter went the extra mile to protect the precious racing skis. It was felt that no part of them should be touching or even very close to the floor."

We all nodded at the logic of going to extremes to protect the invaluable skis.

"First, I examined the steel frame. All of the steel pins had been severed by a metal saw. Next, I was able to find evidence that all of the main wooden supports had been similarly compromised. And finally, the front legs of the rack had been sawn through and a trip wire had been rigged to pull both of them out with very little pressure on the wire."

We were all struggling to believe the level of depravity necessary for this type of destruction. And Tom drew his report to its conclusion.

"Based on some items found behind and under the ski rack, it appears as though the victim had been hiding out behind the rack and for some unknown reason had decided to run around to the front of the rack. Which would have been an insane move if he had been the saboteur. You can guess the rest. He tripped the wire pulling the entire rack and nearly 50 pairs of skis with extremely sharp edges down on top of himself."

Jon then added "I spoke with Officer Bachmann a few minutes ago. He said that everything Tom found matched what they themselves were speculating, but until Tom was able to confirm the details with specific evidence, it was all just guesswork. They were most appreciative that Tom had flown in for a detailed examination of what they were now sure was a crime scene for which they had irrefutable evidence."

After a moment of silence as we all struggled to compute the sordid details that Tom had uncovered, I looked up. At that moment, Dominique looked at me. I could tell by the look in her eyes that we were thinking the exact same thing, it was time to take a deep dive into Beau's background and life in Jim Thorpe, PA.

#####

Dominique and I wasted no time in discussing an immediate action plan. It was decided that I would consult my friends from Pennsylvania about Jim Thorpe and Dominique would circle back to Officer Bachmann for a rundown on Beau's work background and any other related details he would be able to share.

Since Jim Thorpe was fairly close to Philadelphia I knew precisely who to consult. Ironically, in order to get the best information about occurrences on the eastern seaboard, I would have to contact our good friends from over 2,000 miles further west in the mountainous state of Utah. Before retiring to Utah, Gerald and Laura-Nicolas Völlmer had spent the bulk of their professional careers in Philly. And these were the type of people who didn't miss a trick. I was confident they would be able to give me accurate intel, and probably direct me to other invaluable resources.

A quick text to my friends garnered more than I'd hoped for. They were extremely familiar with Jim Thorpe since Laura-Nicolas' Penn State college roommate lived there currently with her husband and three kids. They had stayed in close touch since graduation. In fact, these same friends were due for a visit to Utah within the next month. I had hit pay dirt, big time!

We set a time for a Zoom call the next day at 9 am U.S. Mountain time and I proceeded to work with Dominique to determine all the appropriate questions. I also wanted to obtain permission to contact Laura-Nicolas' former roommate so that I could question her directly.

Dominique had already arranged to meet her officer friend, Hermann for a hot Ovomaltine chocolate at the end of his workday, but the intrigue of learning more about Beau, combined with the prospect of being introduced to 'The Switzerland of America' proved too strong a draw so she called and moved her meeting to lunchtime hoping she'd be able to join my video call.

[Chapter 18]

The next day I spent some time on the computer researching everything I could about Jim Thorpe. I wanted to learn all I could to get a feel for this quaint little town that boasted a Swiss flavor and had apparently emerged from a coal mining history as was fairly common in Pennsylvania. I wanted some context before my Zoom call, but I was also wondering whether I'd be able to pick up any facts relating to Beau himself. If he was sort of a known entity, albeit not the sort of entity I would normally want to research, there might be some stories local to Jim Thorpe that featured him.

By mid-day I had a pretty good feel for why Jim Thorpe had achieved its acclaim, aside from the fact that Mr. Thorpe was the first Native American to win a gold medal in the Olympics. It really is a small world.

I also had a collection of articles outlining the life of the victim, Beau, and believe me, they weren't pretty. Since so much of his time had been spent in Jim Thorpe, the local paper that covered their news, *Time News Online*, managed to follow Beau's infamy throughout the great state of Pennsylvania.

Most of the stories focused on defrauding anyone and anything from his own neighbors, to insurance companies to bankers and there was even one story of his selling bogus pharmaceuticals in various parts of the state. Beau was a real piece of work. Although I am a strong proponent for not speaking ill of the dead, I was pretty sure there was nothing good that anyone would have to say about him. In fact, the most positive part of this investigation was the fact that I would never have to meet Beau. As horrible as that makes me sound, I'm nothing if not a realist. Hmmm. That's probably due to my Swiss heritage!

As I waited for Dominique to return I became aware that the familiar, niggling feeling was back. The more I tried to capture whatever it was about Pennsylvania that was floating around in my brain the more elusive it seemed. Would I ever remember the damn thing? I had a stronger than ever feeling that it would be extremely important. I would just have to let my subconscious do its job since my conscious seemed to be openly mocking me.

#####

Dominique returned from her lunch with Hermann and filled me in on their conversation.

"Hermann will gladly supply us with the names of Beau's employers," she started, "but we're on our own to find out what may have transpired in each case. He should have the list to us within an hour or so."

"That seems fair. Just seeing the list and the dates of employment should begin to paint a picture."

"I agree. But I'm wondering how we will get past employers to share any details of his employment. They will certainly refuse to share reasons why he may have been fired."

"Well, Dominique, here's where investigations can get a bit sticky. It may be necessary to invent the persona of a fictious reporter or possibly an HR professional looking to hire.

Sometimes claiming to be a student doing research… It's never terribly comfortable, but it can be extremely productive.

"Using any of these identities, as a private investigator might do, you can rest assured that no one questioned would be likely to disclose more than the most elementary information. And, as long as we can be certain our queries won't hurt anyone, especially not Beau since he's dead, but will appreciably serve the greater good…

"It would undoubtedly go a long way toward a deeper understanding of our victim, which could be an immeasurable help in advancing the investigation."

"I will tell you right now, Donna, this will be up to you and your team. It would not bode well if I were to be found making phone calls under a false name. I would not be setting the right example."

'You're right Dominique. I sometimes forget that you are always being observed in every part of your life. I too always strive to set the highest ethical example, but since I'm not a celebrity I have just a bit more latitude."

"It's interesting Donna, I had never really thought about where to draw the line on behavior that is not designed to hurt anyone. In fact it is designed to help catch an alleged murderer, but it could be seen as something nefarious if a public figure were to be caught behaving in this way. I have always had to think about never doing anything that could be considered inappropriate, regardless of the motive or outcome. Thinking of it that way, it does seem a bit constricting. But as you say, I would not feel comfortable making such calls anyway. In our world today people are so quick to judge regardless of motive or outcome. It is imperative to stay far north of the line of any perceived impropriety."

Unlike Dominique, I had thought about this issue many times. In the world of advertising, there are minute improprieties that have always made me uncomfortable, but have occurred fairly frequently from my observation. I had consistently refrained from participating in such schemes since most of them could have hurt or compromised others, more in a business sense than in a life threatening way, but still, not acceptable.

Over the years as I prepared media plans for my clients, I would occasionally get a call from someone claiming to be a college student preparing to embark on the creation of a media buying campaign for a fictional project. They would ask me to give them specific details of a plan I had prepared for a specific client – one that they named - to help them understand how to plan their own assignment successfully. At Marcel we have always been eager to help students, but when we received a call asking for one of our client media plans, well that was way too shady. We shut that down in a heartbeat.

In truth, these were never college students. Rather, the calls were from junior folks in competitive agencies in an attempt to obtain key details in order to endeavor to steal the client in question away from our agency.

When they had the intimate details they would pitch the client and attempt to prove they could improve on their budget value. They would set out to illustrate how an approach using a plan such as ours would be a waste of budget dollars. Luckily, these fraudulent attempts were ridiculously transparent and often resulted in embarrassment and a soiled reputation for the agencies attempting such maneuvers.

This was the worst kind of bottom feeding behavior and something no agency I worked for ever tried. This may come as a surprise but not everyone in the ad industry lets ethics get in the way of financial success.

My first experience with such deception, albeit on a much smaller scale, came while I was a junior media person in a Hartford ad agency. Our client was the daily newspaper for the area. My boss asked me if I would call *Connecticut Magazine* and ask for a media kit – with all the details and advertising rates – for our newspaper client. She neglected to mention that she had chosen me for my new employee innocence and that this was a covert mission in which I could not reveal the name of my client.

I made the call and requested the media kit. The sales rep asked me what client I was calling for and I told him. He seemed a little surprised but agreed to send the kit.

When my boss asked about the call and I gave her the details she flipped out and began screaming at me.

"You were asking for competitive information so the paper knows what their competitors charge! Why did you give them the client's name?"

How the hell was I supposed to know that? Maybe if she had mentioned that – but no, this boss was notorious for giving only the barest amount of information to ensure that she was the only one who looked knowledgeable to the senior staff and clients. Suffice it to say that she was not at all popular with her staff and I did not appreciate her using me for her ill-gotten gains. This would not have been a victimless lie.

The *Connecticut Magazine* media kit was easily available to anyone – but this was my first foray into competitive 'espionage' and I learned a valuable lesson that day – to hate that lying can play a key part in business – even for mostly reputable businesspersons. I also learned that, in my remaining career, I should choose never to replicate my boss' behavior – this was not her only shifty maneuver.

[Chapter 19]

The next morning the focus was all on Lyra. Dominique had been fitting in as many sessions with her as possible. She was concerned that the combination of being so involved in a tragic death, and one in which Lyra herself could possibly have been the intended victim, compounded by the loss of her favorite skis, could send Lyra into a doldrum that would be difficult to reverse and thus negatively impact her racing progress.

While some folks might see this as the least of the worries, Dominique was sharp enough to realize that racing progress would be the fastest way to orient Lyra in a positive direction. And clearly, that was critically important in keeping her on track. No one could be left unaffected under this particular set of circumstances. Sadly, Lyra would not be wrong to be worried since the police had not yet ascertained all of the who or any of the why.

Dominique suggested that we use the morning to watch and encourage Lyra as she clocked her time during several practice runs. We wondered if Dominique would suggest a venue other than Titlis, but she felt that Lyra should race on that mountain quickly before too much time had elapsed, and often, so that she did not develop a phobia about that particular mountain and potentially throw her career away.

Short of moving to France or Italy, Lyra would have to be comfortable, even beyond comfortable racing at her home mountain.

Once there it became immediately clear why Dominique had set things up as she had. The activity and excitement, in general around the ski area and also within Lyra's group of supporters would render Lyra hard pressed to wallow in fear or depression.

We watched and cheered as Lyra took each turn with speed and precision. Dominique's face radiated with pride as Lyra's times continued to impress her.

In retrospect, this seemed like a turning point in Dominique's mentoring of Lyra. All along she had been increasingly encouraged by Lyra's drive and determination, but there had been a few lingering doubts. Maybe Lyra was too nice and didn't have enough of a "killer" instinct to truly be a champion. Realizing that Lyra had the ability to shake off all the recent negative events and their implications, not to mention the doom and gloom that her parents still couldn't shake. Seeing her continue to race, while systematically pushing her capabilities beyond their limitations, Dominique could see a true force in the world of ski racing.

It was difficult to imagine, just a couple of days out from tragedy that we could all feel so energized and even euphoric, but life can be funny that way.

By noon we were sporting raw throats from all of the screaming and cheering. We decided to split up the group. Babs and Peg were heading out to hunt ancestry, while the majority of the group chose to change clothes and hit the slopes. Dominique felt this was a critical time to spend with Lyra so she begged off our call.

I excused myself to get back to the apartment in order to jump on my Zoom call with the Völlmers. That was a godsend in more ways than one. I definitely wanted the inside scoop on Jim Thorpe and I was pretty sure I was not ready to hit those Engelberg mountain slopes. Go ahead and think of me as a chicken. I think I'm wise enough to know my limits and respect them. In fact, I respect the hell out of them!

#####

"Donna, it's so good to hear your voice and see your smiling face," the ever cheerful Laura-Nicolas practically sang.

"Yes, Donna, how are you enjoying Switzerland and how was the trip over?" the ever pragmatic Gerald chimed in.

"All good so far, thanks. Well, almost all good as you know, that's why I'm calling. But, one thing I can say, it is more beautiful here than I could have imagined!"

"Yes, we have both spent time in Switzerland while on work assignments. Although most of our time was spent in corporate office buildings, you couldn't help but see the beauty that was all around." Gerald stated.

"And Donna, how are you finding your new relatives?" Laura-Nicolas asked.

"They have been so warm and welcoming, I couldn't have imagined any better reception. And it's been so exciting finally getting to see Lyra race."

"And how is their house…"

"Alright L-N, Donna is calling for a specific purpose. She can give us all the glorious details of her trip once they're back in the states. So Donna, tell us about this murder and how you think we can be of help."

I proceeded to fill them in on all of the details as I knew them.

"…So, getting to know everything we can about this Jones character will help us determine whether or not he was the intended victim."

"Well, Donna," started Laura-Nicolas, "when you first texted us about Beauford "Beau" Jones it rang a bell. I checked with Gerry to see if he felt the same, and he did."

"Yes, in fact he's quite a conversation starter for residents of Jim Thorpe. Even without doing any research Laura-Nicolas' former roommate had filled us in quite a bit on the 'Fumbling Fraudster,' which is the Jim Thorpe nickname for Beau Jones."

"What really makes him a legend in Jim Thorpe," Laura-Nicolas chimed in, "is not the fact that he attempted so very many acts of fraud in various different ways, but the fact that he managed to fumble 100% of his fraudulent attempts. And he has managed to do jail time for many of those attempts."

"You'd think he might have realized that he didn't have an aptitude for fraud or any other criminal activity! Apparently, there is a minimum IQ threshold even for the dumbest crook, and he clearly falls far beneath that," I added.

"Needless to say, our friend Beau has become a legend, he is the "laughing stock of Jim Thorpe." Now that doesn't mean that the residents of this already noteworthy town have any affection for good old Beau. They've just been waiting for him to commit the ultimate fumbled crime that will keep him in jail once and for all," Gerry added.

"He may be a legend in Jim Thorpe, but the prevailing thought is that he is a legendary embarrassment. In fact, we would not have been privy to any of these juicy details if we weren't close to several residents through my former roommate. Oh sure, you can find the newspaper articles outlining his follies and the resulting jail terms – but you don't get the birds eye view of just how he managed to fumble each one if you don't have the right contacts," Laura-Nicolas said.

"Based on your knowledge, so far, do you think Beau would more likely be the fumbling murderer or the murder victim?"

"Well, you know we don't like to speculate without all the facts," Laura-Nicolas was quick to respond.

"True, but just a SWAG, (i.e. Sophisticated Wild Ass Guess) based on his history, if he was trying to commit a murder he obviously bungled it. I mean it would have been the most bungled murder of all times. But considering his rate of failure, I have a hard time believing that he tried to murder someone else and ended up killing himself. That theory seems to give him credit for being able to kill someone even if that someone is himself. And that would be a big step up for him. The simplest and most likely answer is that someone else was trying to murder him. Now the question becomes, did someone from Switzerland kill him and why? Or did someone follow him over to Switzerland to kill him and again why? And finally, why was he in Switzerland in the first place?" Gerry said summing things up.

"All excellent points, and based on your SWAG logic I tend to agree. I think the next step is to try and determine why he was in Switzerland. That should also answer the question of who this alleged murderer was," I commented.

"You know, Donna. If Beau was the murderer and he did bungle the job and ended up killing himself, there is an upside for him," Gerry concluded.

"What's that, Gerry?"

"At least this time he won't go to jail!"

That got a chuckle from me and a massive eye roll from Laura-Nicolas, illustrating once more the benefits of a video call.

We finished up with action steps. Gerry and Laura-Nicolas would continue to work with L-N's college roommate to obtain specific details of where Beau's victim's were located, what various types of fraud he tried to perpetrate and how he bungled each one. They also suggested I speak directly with L-N's roommate, Jean, for any subtle details that she might divulge during the course of a conversation. Laura-Nicolas would contact Jean and let her know I'd be texting. I felt it was a productive debriefing and that I'd have a stellar "feet on the street" team in the U.S.

"Oh Donna, one more thing," Laura-Nicolas added, "Jean is a bit of an acquired taste."

"In what way?"

"Ha," Gerry barked, "you'll have to see it to believe it, Donna."

"Well at least give me something. You can't just leave it like that."

Laura-Nicolas let out a long and slightly unnerving sigh, "she's quite a handful. What you'd call a larger-than-life personality. Not a lot of folks ever get the chance to realize that she is brilliant and caring because the initial shock has them running for cover."

"Oh, well if that's all. Don't forget I've been in advertising for too many years to mention. And you know we're a collection of "interesting characters," many of whom are larger-than-life. I'm sure Jean will prove to be nothing new for me."

"Sure Donna," Gerry added with an obvious smirk (those video calls are not always helpful), "sure."

You have to love those corporate types. They have no idea how the "creative" side of the workforce functions. And trust me, it is usually high emotions on steroids. That is what gets things so energized and makes work so much fun, but it is also what often gets in the way of progress. And when that energy wanes, things go to hell so fast your head will spin. Running a creative agency is a fine balance of supporting the highs without letting them get in the way and recharging when things get low. Neither of which is for the faint of heart.

No, I was not worried about Jean's over-the-top personality. It was something I dealt with on a daily basis. In fact, I think it's fair to say I'm pretty damn good at it, so bring it on!

I filled the rest of the team in on our call that evening over homemade Grüendonschtigsuppe for luck in our investigation. I mean why wouldn't you eat a soup that would give you luck in the months to come?

[Chapter 20]

Over soup, Babs and Peg filled us in on their ancestry hunting for the day. They had visited city halls in a list of little villages that they felt could hold answers to their possible Swiss ancestry. During their search, Peg began to realize that it was more likely her ancestry had originated in Germany. Although this was a mild disappointment, she felt it was reassuring to have a solid lead into her German ancestry.

Babs on the other hand, had managed to find that her Mother's Mother had a father who was born in Basel. Based on her research it appeared that her ancestor was from either Wengen or Grindelwald. Details were a bit fuzzy and she felt one village was the place of birth and the other the place of citizenship. Her next step would be to track down folks in each village in the hope of finding a distant relative.

I'm not entirely sure why these action steps filled me with trepidation.

"Hey Babs, let me know when you're going to try chatting up the villagers. I think I'd like to be there," I offered.

We spent the rest of that evening sharing speculation on what could possibly have happened to cause Beau's murder/accidental death. Tom, who had agreed to stay on for an extra day if he and Jon could form an ad hoc beer tasting tour, had an interesting take on who the murderer could be.

"Based on my in-depth analysis of the damaged materials that had previously been the ski rack, I believe that Beau could definitely have been the murderer."

"Why do you say that, Tom?" Dominique asked.

"Well, simply because every visible attack on the wood and the steel frame in that rack was done the wrong way. I mean there is a way to go about dismantling a rack such as this one – and this murderer did not make one strike with the knowledge of even the most ignorant of DIYers. Everything he did made everything else he did much more difficult. It's a miracle the rack actually did fall apart when the trip wire was triggered and that it didn't collapse on the perpetrator during the act of sabotage. If this weren't a murder investigation I would try to recreate his blunders in a video. I know people who would pay good money for that kind of entertainment!"

#####

The next morning I woke feeling a bit nervous. We were already over a quarter of the way through our vacation and we were not close on solving the mystery. I would have to talk to Jon about extending our stay if we ended the week without any more clear direction. It was all well and good that the victim had been identified. But there were still so many unanswered questions. And the fact remained, if our victim was in fact the murderer, who was the intended victim and was that person still in danger?

I couldn't help but remember how close Lyra had come to being severely injured or even killed but I also couldn't imagine why on earth anyone would want to harm her.

And there it was again, that niggling feeling in the back of my head. It was still just out of reach.

"Good morning, sunshine," Jon's first words of the day.

I have to say, I wasn't feeling much like sunshine. I began to fill Jon in on the thoughts that had been consuming me that morning.

"I know what happened, and why," Jon stated bluntly, "I've written it down and asked Will to put it in their family safe. He has agreed not to read it."

"You know?"

"Yep."

"And you're not going to tell me?"

"Nope, oh and Tom agrees with me."

"But Jon…wait, you told Tom?"

"He's heading home tomorrow and I know I can trust him to keep my secret. And before those wheels start turning, there is no amount of beer that will get Tom to divulge this secret so don't even try."

"Hmmmf."

"I believe in you and Dominique. Right now, what I know is purely conjecture and will only serve to frustrate the both of you. You're headed in the right direction and that's all I'll say. When you both arrive at the conclusion, you will have evidence that will be necessary to support the action steps that will have to be taken."

Well, damn, I couldn't exactly argue with that.

"And furthermore, I know you both well enough to know my conclusion will just throw you off track. You're both too stubborn to believe anyone else without tons of proof."

He had me there.

[Chapter 21]

After breakfast the group split. Jon and Tom headed out on their beer tour, Dominique and Lyra hit the slopes to ski and train as well as re-interview some of the mountain staff to see if they remembered any additional details after having had time to reflect. Peg, Babs and I headed into the villages from whence Babs may have originated.

Before heading out I spoke with Dominique for any last-minute words of advice.

"Perhaps the three of you would be better off touring the pubs with Jon and Tom."

Yeah, I kind of saw that coming.

"Have you ever tried to stop a freight train, Dominique?"

"Good point. If you go to the town hall, ask for introductions to key people. Approach with deference and formality – do not charge in like the bull in the china shop! You can also ask in a restaurant or pub for an introduction to well-known customers. If anyone does not appear pleased with your request, apologize immediately and get out of there! I will think positive thoughts – you will need all you can get. But let me say that I am quite happy not to have been invited on this expedition."

"Well, here goes nothing."

"You can say that again, Donna."

With the benefit of Dominique's car we three started out on our perilous mission – perilous mostly to our own self confidence.

Since Wengen does not permit cars, we were forced to park in Lauterbrunnen and take the train into Wengen. By the time we reached the little village it was evident these folks spoke enough English that we would be able to communicate easily.

On the train we learned that we must take the time to check out Jungfrau as it is one of the most spectacular mountains in the Swiss Alps. We made a mental note not to leave the village without taking a look. We determined that our sightseeing would have to wait until we'd made some headway in our research. After that we could take the train to Jungfraujoch in order to enjoy the magnificent views of Jungfrau.

From the congenial train ride to Wengen, we were starting to feel as though maybe the folks here would not be so closed off and formal. They were very forthcoming with extremely helpful tips about what not to miss and where to eat. We all started to feel more relaxed and optimistic.

Then, I could hear Dominique in my head "Do not make the mistake of thinking that people who are polite and friendly to tourists in order to help them enjoy their visit will also be as open to personal questions about specific citizens and their ancestry. These are two very different situations and will be dealt with very differently. If you start to ask these helpful folks your specific questions, you will find that the formality will soon appear and then you will get little or no information from them. You might even find that you have offended them."

Dammit, how did she keep getting in my head? That was really starting to freak me out. But, freaky or not, that was probably very good advice from Dominique and it helped me readjust my whole demeanor and my determination to keep Babs and Peg from getting us all into hot water.

After a brief, whispered reminder about the need for formality to Babs and Peg, two women who had lived their lives using little or no formality, our train arrived in the Wengen station where we asked to be directed to the town hall or equivalent so that our search could begin in earnest.

On the walk over we could see that Wengen itself was a charming and authentic Swiss village with breathtaking mountain views. I could see right away that I would be happy just spending the day strolling around and checking out the view from all angles. But that's not why we were here, and I had to respect Babs' mission and help her try to locate her ancestors.

We arrived at the "official" building or, Gemeindehaus as it is known in Swiss villages, and entered the main office. The women there directed us to an office in the back of the second floor where information on births and citizenships were documented.

There sat an elderly gray-haired woman with pince nez hanging from a chain around her neck. She was dressed in a long and ill-fitting pencil skirt and a heavy cable knit sweater. It was difficult to tell if she was tiny or huge. She looked up as we entered and immediately assumed the look of someone smelling a rotten egg.

There we stood with our all-black fitted slacks and button-down shirts, with our not too terrible menopausal bodies – ready for business.

"I can help you with something?" she barked.

I could feel the sweat begin to form on my forehead wondering if it would be at all possible to turn this into a positive encounter. But Babs and Peg were in no way daunted.

"We're looking for folks with the last name of Schmid, will we find them in Wengen," started Babs.

"Certainly you will," Pince-nez replied, "which Schmid family?"

"Well," Peg joined in, "we're not entirely sure, we'll have to do some more research…"

"Then come back when you do know." snapped Pince-nez.

And as quickly as that, we were dismissed.

"But," Babs managed before Peg and I grabbed her arms and dragged her out of the office and down the hall.

"Let's take what we've just learned and apply it somewhere else for additional information," stated Peg in her school marm voice.

As we moved down the hall we observed a door marked 'Residential.' We all stopped and turned toward the door.

Inside was a lovely young woman with wavey auburn hair and a teal-colored sweater dress that hugged her curves in all the right places. Her smile was as lovely as the rest of her.

And we, still sporting our fitted black and quasi-passible menopausal selves.

"Welcome, I am Elke, and how may I help you on this lovely day?"

"Hello Elke," we all chimed in.

"We are searching for residences inhabited by a Schmid family," Peg took the lead.

"Well then you are in luck. We have a directory with all the residences in Wengen, and the surname is shown. Feel free to have a look and use one of those desks in the corner."

Score! We thankfully received the directory and headed over to the tables. Luckily, with a village as small as Wengen, there were only a handful of Schmids and we took photos of each address.

"Okay let's go."

"Go where," I asked.

"Check out all the Schmid residences for my ancestors, where else?"

"Now hold on. Didn't you hear anything I told you about Dominique's advice? We can't just go charging around to various residences without something of a formal introduction."

"Well, where will we get that?" Peg demanded.

Apparently, Elke had witnessed our little disagreement and she interjected her thoughts. "I agree with the blonde-haired lady. It would not be at all appropriate for you to go charging up to residences with no attempt at any protocol necessary for a welcome reception. Now let's think this through together. Let me see your list and I will do what I can to give you a proper introduction."

This woman was a godsend. Without her input I could picture myself wrestling both Peg and Babs to keep them from causing a gaffe that could indubitably keep Babs away from any relatives she might still have in Wengen. We took a moment to explain our plight to Elke to assure her of our honorable intentions.

With Elke's help we determined that she herself could give us an entrée to five of the Schmid families. And she felt that one or two of her friends and associates might know a few more. There were, however, several families to whom an introduction would not be forthcoming.

After a few hours, Elke was able to confirm that we could eliminate ten Schmid families from our inquiries. And while that was disappointing, it did save us an enormous amount of time and effort.

When all was said and done, only five Schmid families were unknown to Elke and her resources. We thanked Elke profusely and offered to buy her lunch, which she politely declined, so we headed out of the administrative building.

Once outside Babs declared "Okay, let's get a map and hit the first address!"

"Seriously?"

"I'm here now and I may never be back, so let's do this!"

#####

Four of the Schmid residences appeared to be empty. Not terribly surprising in the middle of a working and school day. And we certainly didn't want to appear with questions and no introduction to a house with school kids waiting for their parents to arrive home after work. That could truly prove disastrous.

Our luck changed on the fifth house. Although no one answered when we rang the doorbell, we did hear some banging that sounded as if it came from the back of the house. It was as though Babs had grown wings. She flew toward the noise with Peg and I attempting to keep up.

And there, at the back of the Schmid property, was an outbuilding. And working on that outbuilding was a gentleman of about 50 years of age.

"Hello, Sir," Babs started, "Can I ask you a few questions?"

"Who are you and why are you on my property?"

Oh Lord, here we go!

"We are terribly sorry to invade your privacy, Herr Schmid," I interjected.

"How do you know my name?"

Shit. That was probably stupid on my part.

After a few minutes of apologizing and explaining, Herr Schmid was nice enough to entertain Babs' questions. It didn't take long before we learned that the Wengen Schmid's were probably not the ones related to Babs. Disappointing, but we were homing in on Grindelwald as the most likely place of Babs' origin.

As we were thanking Herr Schmid for his help and insights and apologizing once again, Babs' attention was directed toward the project that had drawn us into the back in the first place.

"So Herr Schmid," Babs started, "it looks to me like you're trying to shore up this old building by adding a beam to the one that looks split and cracked."

"That is correct Frau Babs, but it seems my ability to complete this project on my own has been mere folly and I will have to wait until my brother-in-law returns from his ski trip in order to get the help I will need."

"Not at all," Babs continued with a huge grin, "I've flipped many a house and I am ready, willing and able to give you all the help you need."

"Oh, I think not, Frau Babs, I would not ask you to do such a thing."

"I insist!" She pushed as Peg and I shared a look of sheer horror.

"Babs, maybe…"

"Let's get started!"

So they did.

Babs and Herr Schmid each climbed a ladder positioned on either side of the large single room. With each step up it was clear from Babs' face that this beam was far heavier than any she had experienced. Peg and I just held our breath and stood out of the way.

As Herr Schmid began to force the beam up into place on his side, there was a minor shift in balance. It was just enough for Babs to lose her footing and consequently her grip on the beam. Within seconds, Babs began to fall, but the beam fell faster, knocking Herr Schmid off his ladder and cracking him on the head before either hit the ground. And then we heard the crash. The first one caused by the beam shooting through the window on Herr Schmid's side and the second from the beam shooting up and cracking the proposed sister beam in half once and for all.

Luckily, Herr Schmid's head injury was not as bad as the excessive bleeding would indicate and we were all able to scramble out of the building seconds before the roof collapsed entirely.

In the minutes following the incident we phoned for emergency help for Herr Schmid amid his minor protestations. We cleaned up most of the blood and helped him assess the damage. We also checked Babs, but miraculously, she once again emerged unscathed.

"Oh Herr Schmid, I am so sorry," Babs sung her familiar tune.

"It is okay, Frau Babs. For a long time I have been debating whether to fix this old broken down building or take it down and build another. You have helped to make this choice for me…"

I looked over at Babs' beaming face (no pun intended) and just shook my head. She is the only woman I know who can take down a building and emerge a hero – at least in her own mind.

As the first responders were pulling away, and we began our good-byes with Herr Schmid, the ambulance stopped and the driver rolled down the window.

"Oh, by the way, we heard from the administrative building and they've asked us to give you folks a message. They would prefer that you end your visit in Wengen earlier than planned, and perhaps that you not return."

I wish this was a shock and something new for us. Sadly, it was not. We agreed to head directly to the train to Lauterbrunnen and the car. Perhaps we would try to see Jungfrau on a subsequent trip with Dominique to keep us on point, with the three of us wearing deep disguise.

[Chapter 22]

We got back to the flat just as Dominique and Lyra were arriving from their training morning. One look at our faces told Dominique there was a story to tell.

"Are you going to fill us in or do we have to interrogate you?"

So we proceeded to tell Dominique and Lyra about our morning in Wengen. Once things got intense Lyra just laughed and laughed. Dominique was another story. Her expressionless face went from white to pale green to about a puce color – it was actually pretty cool. Just about at the time when her face settled down to slightly ashen she shared her thoughts – or maybe we overheard her private thoughts.

"Yes, of course, what would I expect? Did I not warn them well enough, do they ever listen to anyone?" she mumbled.

After about 5 minutes of what sounded like Dominique berating herself, she faced us ready to have a conversation.

"Perhaps we will rethink any further excursions for Babs and Peg. It occurs to me that heavy supervision, and possibly disguises, make the most sense."

"Well I…"

"You know, Donna, you are perilously close to the Gefahrenzone yourself, you need to think more carefully next time, you're giving me major Kopfschmerzen!"

I guess it's easier to revert to one's native language when under duress. To the great surprise of many, I knew when it was time to shut up!

Dominique was able to move on fairly quickly even though it was obvious actions (mostly Babs' actions) of that morning had clearly been a concern.

"Now let me fill you in on what I learned this morning as Lyra and I made our way around the Engelberg mountain in an immensely productive training experience."

Lyra was beaming from ear to ear. It was clear her thinking was in lock step with Dominique.

"I tried to find staff to question at each level of the mountain. I felt that within a few days of the murder at least some of them would have thought of anything unusual that may have occurred. I really hit it big when we were in and around Stand. One of the ski patrol was checking the area for any problems. He is someone I have known for a while so we exchanged a greeting.

I asked him how things had been since the incident and he proceeded to describe the heightened level of security that management had felt was necessary, at least until more of their questions had been answered. Then I asked him where he had been that morning and he said.

"Now that you ask, I have remembered I was just in this spot 20 minutes before the big crash was heard. I did see something that had me puzzled. There was an American…"

I asked, "how did you know he was an American?" He just gave me a look. We both laughed and he continued.

128

"He was an American, but he was wearing the staff jacket that we all use. He was walking across Stand to the building where the ski rack was located but there were no skis in sight. It did not occur to me at the time that this could well have been the victim – or the perpetrator as well as the victim."

I thanked him for his information and suggested he speak to the police. He agreed and rushed off to find the detective.

"Dominique, that's huge!"

We were all blown away by this important discovery. When Jon and Tom got back from their beer tasting exploits we filled them in on everything. Jon smiled and nodded as though he'd known about the American in the "borrowed" mountain jacket all along. And damn him, he probably had!

In addition to Dominique's important discovery and Babs' deconstruction of a building as well as our reputation, Jon and Tom had met a few real characters in their travels so it was like one big party. We invited the rest of the Bryner family over and we all ate pizza and shared our stories. We were having the best time!

As the evening waned it became clear that Babs and Peg had a real yearning to attempt skiing in Switzerland, in earnest. Even though their initial foray, on the day of the accident, ended up more about them being carried by the mountain guides than either of them implementing skis on snow. I would have to make sure they understood that their next attempt would be sans chiseled-faced guides.

After much discussion, it was decided that we would all head over to Andermatt in the morning and would ski over to

Sedrun for some nice cruising runs. Dominique and Jon agreed to spend the morning on the novice area teaching Babs and Peg. I would ski in and around that area, sometimes with them and sometimes in a slightly more aggressive area. The rest of the group would choose their preferred areas based on their own skill levels and we would all meet up for lunch.

Once we reached Andermatt we made our way over to Sedrun on skis, some of us less on skis than on butts and knees. Before scattering to the various areas we shared brief explanations of where we would be, just in case, and we agreed on a time and place to meet for lunch.

I was thoroughly enjoying myself. I could weave around between the easiest of areas watching Dominique and Jon try to get two menopausal midwestern women to look graceful on skis – frankly, it made me feel like a pro and a little boost to the ego is always a welcome thing – especially post menopause!

With extremely exact directions from Dominique I was able to venture out into some of the slightly more difficult runs and then back to the novice area when my legs were looking for a break.

I could tell Dominique was impressed with the fortitude of my two team members. They were Nebraska farm strong and not afraid of anything. Having taught more than his share of menopausal women, Jon was critical in being able to intuit their needs and issues and address them before any problem could arise.

Sedrun had a fairly extensive novice area with some t-bars and a couple of chairlifts. They all fed off of one main t-bar that went right up the middle. My first concern, and I'm sure it was Jon's as well, was the difficulty of getting anyone prepared for the balancing act a t-bar required. Added to that was the concern that t-bars in Europe are not at all like t-bars in the U.S. In the U.S. t-bars are on hills that are usually very flat. In Europe they can be so steep that you feel as though you're scaling a skyscraper – they can be unimaginably steep. The main t-bar here was unquestionably a European t-bar.

Both Jon and Dominique gave excruciatingly detailed instructions to Babs and Peg. And much to their surprise, the pair made it up the t-bar first time with no fatalities – or even injuries. That was a huge relief, and kind of a shock to their instructors, especially since neither of them had remained upright on skis for more than one turn during their first attempt on the slopes.

After that, with an iron will, they continued to impress and delight both Dominque and Jon with their resilience. Don't get me wrong, they were not going to win any medals. And there was no fear of wearing out the rental skis since they rarely touched the snow, causing me to ask myself 'is it possible to teach an old dog new tricks?'

On the other hand, I was having a quite different experience. I couldn't remember the last time I'd had this much fun on the slopes. Free to roam to whatever skill level appealed to me in the moment, and looking damn good whenever I ventured into the easiest area. Everybody was smiling, we were all having fun. What were we all so concerned about?

Doesn't it always happen that, whenever you stop and think "things are great, I've got nothing to worry about," that something happens? Well, if it doesn't, you're not me!

Babs and Peg headed up the t-bar in front of Jon and Dominique for what seemed like the millionth time – and everything was fine. They got to the top and the menopausal first timers were clearly feeling full of themselves. They were killing it on the t-bar. Once back at the top of the novice area they relaxed a bit and began to look around.

"You know," Peg commented, "I've been so focused on learning these new skills and not killing myself that I haven't even had a chance to get a good look at these lovely surroundings."

"I know what you mean, Peg," Babs concurred, "it's lovely here and I'm just seeing that. I'm also fascinated by how this dang t-bar functions. I've never seen any equipment quite like this – as she moved closer to the operations."

The rest of us took a minute for a much-appreciated break. It was so lovely. You could stand and look at the view forever and never get bored. Jon and Dominique took a minute to discuss the progress of their students, or lack thereof. They also wanted to explain the importance of the snowplow stance to Peg. So many students think that once they graduate to parallel skiing the snowplow is never to be used again, but more seasoned skiers know that the snowplow can be a lifesaver in certain situations.

So optimistic of Dominique, when the question rolling around in my head was 'will these two ever have a chance to even use a snowplow?' I know, it sounds really mean, which is why I never voiced this thought – but I was pretty sure it was evident on my face.

Just as we were getting ready to head back down the hill we heard a loud metallic screeching sound and we all turned our heads to Babs who was still standing near the operations.

"What…"

"I just, you know, it looked like it didn't belong there, you know with it just dangling there and everything."

Oh no! Babs!

The next thing we knew lift operators were running all over the area. And the t-bar was not moving. Oh lord, what fresh hell was this? They moved Babs out of the way and frantically went to work trying to get the operations to start operating again.

"Babs, dare I ask," I ventured.

"Well, Donna…"

At this point, there was a crowd forming around Babs, including some of the lift technicians who appeared to have given up on the t-bar. They were anxiously awaiting an explanation that might help to inform them of what they were up against. So, Babs continued.

"Well, you know Peg and I were starting to look around at the mountains and such. And you know me, I am always fascinated by anything mechanical – and the t-bar was like nothing I've ever seen."

She stopped here and smiled. No one returned her smile so she continued.

"So, I was looking at the mechanism that makes the t-bar run and I saw this chain looking out of place and hanging down from the motor. And honestly, I could tell if that chain should get caught up in the cogs and wheels it could screw up the whole system and maybe the t-bar would break down."

"You thought that did you?" Peg growled.

"Well, yeah. So, I grabbed onto that chain and gave it a good yank to get it out of the way completely. And it just broke off in my hand."

At that point the technicians and the lift operators all looked on in horror. Uncertain as to the extent of the problem, Dominique, Jon, Peg and I still looked on in fearful anticipation.

"So that's probably good that I got that dangerous hanging chain out of the way!"

She had gone too far.

"Out of the way?!" The head tech screeched, "out of the way?! That 'dangerous hanging chain' was the safety mechanism without which this, the main t-bar for this whole area, cannot run, it will not turn on!"

"Well, but surely you must have a replacement," Babs continued unwisely.

"There is no replacement."

Now there were faces of horror all around.

"We have never needed a replacement! We have no idea how long it will take to get a replacement, das ist sehr schlecht! Wir haben geschlossen!"

At that point, the rest of the techs and the lift operators moved together to help their colleague clear out of the area and the ski patrol had arrived to ensure that everyone in the novice area would ski to the bottom and head home.

"Well, I guess it's a good thing I discovered that the security chain was in need of replacement, huh?"

All of our eyes and all of the eyes around us turned to glare at Babs.

"Don't even try to convince us that you are a hero!" an indignant Peg responded, "I mean for a minute I thought we were here to do some sightseeing and see Lyra progress in her ski racing career. I guess I forgot we were here to watch you take Switzerland apart, one piece at a time!"

I had a feeling we wouldn't be enjoying a lovely lunch on the mountain today.

[Chapter 23]

Once back at the flat, I felt it would be necessary to hunker down and focus on the investigation. Laura-Nicolas' former roommate, Joan, had agreed to a video chat with me later in the day. Dominique was excited about the prospect of joining me on the call. A friendly interrogation into anything and everything Joan knew about Jim Thorpe and possibly even Beauford Jones would be our focus.

We took a few moments prior to the call to create a list of questions for Joan. The last thing we wanted to do was waste precious time with someone who could be a valuable resource. Dominique and I both knew the odds of our sticking to a set list of questions was unlikely. We were both pretty good shooting from the hip and following the trail of information or even evidence.

One of the pet peeves I've had for years is when a researcher, or a sales person, follows a line of rote questions far after the nature of the conversation has suggested they lead in the wrong direction. In research, sales or even interrogation the need to be able to pivot on a dime is essential for the best possible outcome. That strategy works in communication as well as skiing.

We settled into our video call after introductions. It was immediately clear that Laura-Nicolas had not exaggerated about her friend's over-the-top communication style.

"Oh Dominique, this has to be one of the greatest thrills of my lifetime! I just never thought in all the world that I would be video conferencing with an honest to goodness Olympic gold medal winner! Holy-moly I'm bustin' a gut here! The girls will never believe me in a month of Sundays!"

"That is kind of you, Joan."

"Oh, you must hear that all the time, I'm probably just a great big stupid boring old lady wastin' your valuable time."

"On the contrary. I always appreciate a gracious compliment."

"And you are just so lovely I wish I was there I'd give you a great big old bear hug! Oh my lord, I am just sure I must be the luckiest person alive!"

I was beginning to think we would never get to the subject at hand. Although I could hardly blame Joan for being star struck. Luckily, Dominique had a lot of experience finding a courteous way to redirect the conversation. Although I knew she wasn't bored, I also knew she would find a way to downplay the situation whenever fans began to treat her like royalty.

"As are you, Joan. Donna and I are quite anxious to learn the many things I'm told you want to share with us about Jim Thorpe and Beau Jones. We want to be respectful of your time as a valuable resource.

You know one thing we really need you to enlighten us on is that a policeman friend of mine was going to send me a list of Jones' former employers, and he got back to me and said there were none. Can that possibly be true?"

"Of course!" And just like that I caught a marked shift in Joan's vocal tonality. She had instantly evolved from a star-struck fan to a highly professional researcher, with a fair bit of pumped up ego, after just one comment from Dominique. Huh, and I thought I was good. "That career criminal never held an honest job in his life.

"Let's start from the beginning, shall we? Jones grew up in a problematic family. I mean far more problematic than most. His father never really connected in a career, partly because he kept taking breaks to commit burglary, etc. and ended up in prison two or three times. His mother's main career was being waited on hand and foot by her three kids while whining about her good for nothing husband. Beau was the oldest, so he was sent out to "find" money when meals started to get few and far between. So, his family was well known, and not well liked. Getting any kind of a legitimate job was virtually impossible for Beau."

Dominique and I just shook our heads sadly as we considered the challenges Beau had clearly faced. Joan continued.

"The positive thing about Beau – if there was a positive – was that he knew there was a better way to earn than petty theft. That's when he discovered fraud. And damn if he wasn't good at it. He was a natural. Unfortunately, he was not gifted intellectually so he would set up a sting with all the requisite parts and pieces. He would start the ball rolling brilliantly, but he would invariably stumble badly before bringing his hoax to a close – every single time!"

"So, he spent a lot of time in jail?"

"On and off. Sadly, for Beau, he became extremely well known by the police not just in Pennsylvania, but in a region much larger, as well as the FBI. He had started by targeting the Swiss community in Jim Thorpe thinking he could fool immigrants much faster than those born and bred in the U.S. Whether or not that would be true we may never know, since he never managed to bring any of these scams to a successful conclusion. And unlike other folks who learn from their mistakes, Beau just tried for bigger and better and he failed bigger each time."

"What kind of things did he do?"

"One of his early scams was to convince the Swiss immigrants that he had access to a boat that could bring a large number of their family members over to join them at a fraction of what that kind of journey would normally cost. Naturally, these hard working folks were eager to get their relatives here as quickly as possible, and not spend years apart while working to earn the hefty amounts of money necessary to bring them to the U.S. Family is so important to folks of Swiss origin in particular. His idea generated a great deal of excitement from the Swiss community, and he was just about to collect a great deal of money from over 30 families in and around Jim Thorpe when the bottom fell out of his whole scam.

"Two of the elders within the Swiss community asked to visit Beau's boat. Still thinking he could outsmart everyone, Beau drove them to a large beautiful boat moored in a yacht club outside of Philly. He bribed the guard to give him access and proudly welcomed the two elders aboard. From accounts shared after his arrest, the elders were immediately suspicious when Beau clearly didn't know the way around his own ship. But it didn't come to a head (no pun intended) until the vessel was boarded by the Captain and First Mate for a final inspection before launching on a two-week cruise around the Caribbean.

"That little excursion cost our friend Beau a good eight years behind bars. And it really never got any better after that."

"But Joan, how," I began.

"Does that give us a reason for Beau to be killed in a Swiss ski area?" finished Dominique.

We looked at each other – great minds!

"I really couldn't say," started Joan and both Dominique and I felt immediately deflated. "But there is a rumor going around that Beau had finally given up on his failed fraudulent attempts and was trying something new, something he felt would be equally as lucrative."

What on earth?

"Now remember, this is just a rumor, but word is going around that Beau has decided to go into undercover ops and stealth investigating."

Our minds were racing frantically. Could he have been sent to Switzerland, and more specifically a Swiss ski area, to follow someone? And could his penchant for failure have once again reared its inevitable head leading him into his new career and ending the pain once and for all by having him kill himself accidentally? We knew with no scruples that Beau was likely to be quick to resort to bodily harm if his efforts were thwarted.

We all three talked at once. It was a verbal pinata spilling all over everything.

"That's why…"

"It makes total sense…"

"But remember now, it's just a rumor…"

"It all ties together…"

"OMG, how could we miss that…"

"Joan," Dominique finally got focused, "we can't thank you enough, this call has been incredibly enlightening."

"Oh well, I am just so happy that I've been able to help in your investigation, now don't hesitate to call me if you need anything else, or just say the word and I will fly right out there, if I'm this helpful you need me on sight! In fact, why don't I go on ahead and book a flight, I'll probably stay at your house Dominique, that seems best!"

We took the time to assure Joan that although she had supplied a key piece of information, we did not need her to fly to Switzerland – yet. And then we signed off to ponder what we had learned. And still that niggling feeling pinged at the back of my head.

[Chapter 24]

Dinner that night was a combination of a good-bye party for Tom and a revelation of the intel we'd received from Joan earlier that day on our video call. Because Tom had worked so closely with the polizei while in Switzerland, we had invited Officer Bachmann, and a few of his colleagues to join us for our farewell dinner.

It appeared as though, in between his work with the polizei, Tom had managed to hoist a few beers with them. This was a bond that would not be altered by the miles, and oceans, in between. It was good to see how many different ways one could form lasting bonds. And we knew from past experience that both hops and grapes – along with food of course, we're not animals – were among the best ways.

During our meal, Dominique and I filled everyone in on our conversation with Joan. We mentioned the rumor about the possibility of Beau being a self-proclaimed undercover henchman, and everyone in the room mentally fell into step immediately – except for Jon and Tom who were grinning smugly.

To a person we all knew that Beau had been a hired thug sent to a ski area in Switzerland to make his move. We also instinctively realized that, true to his reputation, Beau had once again screwed up his intended assignment. Only this time it had gotten him killed.

Now we knew who the intended killer was and where he had planned his undercover operation – no more speculation!

We also knew when he had planned to commit some form of bodily harm and how he thought he'd do it. What we still needed to learn was who had hired him and who they had wanted him to harm. But we were so much closer.

Even though we had no idea who had been Beau's intended victim, the fact that the where and how were at a racing ski rack on the Engelberg mountain just prior to a race greatly narrowed the field for us to find the intended victim. The most difficult part of this enormous discovery was that it was most likely the intended victim was a young ski racer. That put us all into a somber mood, especially the Bryners.

The dinner ended with a solid two-pronged action plan: identify the intended victim and keep the young racers safe. And that would be easier said than done.

The next morning we drove Tom to the train with an agreement that we would all come back to vacation here sometime during the next ski season. Heck, now that we'd met Dominique in person and knew our relatives here – I could see us making many more journeys back to Switzerland. We had tried to convince Tom to stick around for a special wine-tasting extravaganza we were hoping to get scheduled, but his response was to be expected 'Call me when you plan a beer tasting dinner.'

As we waved good-bye to Tom, Jon suggested:

"Donna, I think it's time we extended our stay. There's been great progress on the mystery – but there is a lot more work to be done."

Once back at the flat, Jon proceeded to extend our stay by another two weeks. Our dog sitters were thrilled to have the extra time with Frank and Ellie.

As Jon made the necessary arrangements for our extended stay, Dominique and the polizei were at Titlis working on an amped up safety plan for the ski racers.

With Dominique's knowledge of racer needs and likely movements, the polizei would be able to formulate a plan to ensure their safety from anyone and everyone not in the ski racing industry.

Babs and Peg were out sightseeing on their own. They had not yet determined if they were going to extend their stay.

So, I was alone. Neither Jon nor Dominique needed my help and I was a bit too jumpy to relax and sightsee. Now that we'd made some clear progress in determining part of Beau's mission, we couldn't afford to waste any time in identifying his assigned target. We needed to know which racer was in jeopardy and we needed to know who had hired Beau and for what purpose? I could feel the hair on my arms and the back of my neck sticking out.

I decided to go back to Beau's geographical source, Jim Thorpe, PA, and try to find a hint of a clue. I even broadened my search to all of Pennsylvania since Beau's nefarious dealings had extended beyond the borders of Jim Thorpe.

After three hours of poking around on the internet, I finally had that minor light bulb moment and remembered at least some of what had been niggling around in my memory banks. There were multiple connections between Jim Thorpe and Switzerland, and there were several connections between Pennsylvania and Switzerland, but the one that jumped out of the screen at me was the fact that there were a number of large corporations potentially using undercover agents in order to obtain competitive information. Had 'off the radar' Beau been enlisted for some good old corporate espionage?

Pennsylvania housed a sizeable number of large corporations and Swiss companies were no slouch in several of these areas. Finally, after days of driving myself crazy that amorphous thought in the back of my mind had begun working itself out to front and center! We needed to take a close look at the corporate world to see if there was a connection to Beau and to see if there was a dangerous connection to any of the ski racers. Maybe Beau had been hired to keep one of the racers from being a spokesperson for a Swiss corporation. That really didn't seem all that far-fetched. Especially if any of these racers had been doing sponsorships. It was definitely worth checking out!

We would have to take a look at competitive companies in Pennsylvania and Switzerland. Will himself could be my eyes and ears into pharma in Switzerland. Perhaps once we narrowed down the industry it would help to identify the intended victim. I couldn't rule out the possibility that one of the well-meaning Swiss citizens of Jim Thorpe could have helped make that deadly connection for Beau.

It seemed feasible that a U.S. corporation would have hired Beau. But, why on earth would anyone want to hurt a young Swiss ski racer. That didn't make much sense – yet. At least we had a solid lead to follow.

I would have to go back to Gerry and Laura-Nicolas and/or Joan to try to find any inside details. I was sure that Dominique would want to be part of this discussion, so I set up a time for a video chat with Gerry and Laura-Nicolas when I knew Dominique would be available.

Babs and Peg returned from their sightseeing practically bubbling over with excitement. They had decided to try their luck in Grindelwald from a tourist standpoint in order to check out the city before homing in on any possible relatives of Babs. Their elation was due to the fact that they'd had a perfectly wonderful day, saw some exquisite sights and didn't even have one run in with the polizei. They talked about Glacier Canyon – Gletscherschlucht as well as the toboggan run at Pfingstegg. They had lunched at the Avocado Bar and the food was fabulous. Clearly they had made great strides, I was so proud of them!

"So Donna," Peg asked, "do you think you could come back with us sometime this week so we can begin our ancestry investigation?"

Shoot, how did I not see this coming? We've already discovered quite a bit. Even the fact that Babs' relatives were not the Schmid family, but a family distantly related to the Schmid family.

"Well, sure, and if we're lucky maybe we can convince Dominique to join us." I was pretty sure she was booked all week – but it was worth a shot!

Before heading home, Dominique stopped in to tell us about the safety plan they had created for the racers that day. She was very excited and was even thinking these precautions might become a regular part of the Engelberg mountain as well as other ski mountains in Switzerland that regularly featured racing. I hated to think that such a plan was necessary but the past 20 years have taught us that you can't be too careful!

I was then able to fill the group in on my encouraging discovery. Dominique was the first to react.

"Of course, how did we not think of this sooner?"

I looked over and Jon just smiled and nodded. I knew this was a major link to connect even more of the dots in our investigation. And Dominique was eager to join in my video chat with Gerry and Laura Nicholas in about an hour.

[Chapter 25]

We greeted Gerry and Laura-Nicolas and proceeded to explain our sudden interest in corporations in PA. Although they had limited personal knowledge of how likely it would be that a corporation would want to hurt or even kill a ski racer in Switzerland, they understood why our knowledge and research had brought us to this juncture.

"You know, Donna, we've done some IT work for most of the large corporations in PA at various times in our careers, and we wouldn't be able to discuss our work but neither of us encountered any kind of nefarious dealings of any kind." Gerry was quick to explain.

"Oh no, I wouldn't expect that you would, Gerry. I'm not sure what we hope to find, that's why we wanted to chat with you and see if you have any suggestions for how we should move forward with this."

"Well," Laura Nicholas jumped in, "let us give this some thought. We'll put an action plan together to see if we can help pinpoint the most likely suspects.

"Awesome! And thanks."

We chatted for a few more minutes. Dominique and the Völlmers were becoming good friends and I was pretty sure their next big trip would be to Engelberg. It was just a hunch.

After we hung up, Dominique and I spent some time discussing what we did hope to learn from the Völlmer's detective work. It would be too good to be true that we'd find a disgruntled ex-employee who would be quick to say "Oh, yes, my company had many people neutralized if they got in the way – and I was the one who had to obtain the cash in order to pay the depraved scoundrels." No, that was not a likely outcome and we had to realize that even the most disgruntled employee might not be able to be forthcoming with anything other than some vague knowledge of corporate espionage. What were the odds we'd find a whistleblower? But, it didn't hurt to dream!

Before heading home Dominique had one more piece of intel to share.

"Donna, at the risk of alarming you, I think you should know that I am fairly certain I am being followed."

"What!? Why!?"

"I have noticed a woman dressed in such a way that she would typically blend into the background, but her covert movements were impossible for me to ignore. I have seen her several times and it appears as though she is most visible when you and I are together."

"Could she be an autograph seeker looking for the right time to approach you?"

"While that is not outside the realm of possibility, she behaves in a way that no autograph seeker ever has and my instinct tells me she is in some way connected to this investigation."

"Oh shoot, Dominique, this puts a whole new spin on things. I never meant to put you in harm's way, nor did I want to put myself in harm's way, again."

"Donna, this is not something you caused."

"But I should have…."

"Don't Donna. The main thing is that we have identified a potential danger and we will proceed accordingly. I have set up an appointment with my polizei friend, Hermann for first thing in the morning. You and I will go together to fill him in and to learn what action steps must be taken for our safety. And Donna, don't for a moment think that you talked me into partnering with you on this investigation. Ever since Jon and I became friends and I learned of your penchant to investigate murders, I have secretly hoped that we would someday get the chance to work together in an investigation. I did not expect it to happen this time in this way, but that's life."

We said our good-byes and made plans to meet up first thing the next day. In this moment of quiet I had the chance to contemplate what this could possibly mean. My own instincts, along with Dominique's, were sending a clear message: this woman was absolutely a part of this investigation and it was likely she was up to no good. The fact that she clearly had Dominique and me in her headlights sent a solid shiver down my spine and back up again.

On further consideration, it occurred to me that perhaps she was with the Swiss polizei and was assigned to babysit us. After all, Dominique is a national treasure and her close proximity to such a heinous crime would likely make officials in Switzerland feel the need to take precautionary measures, at least until the crime was solved.

Yes, the more I thought about this possibility the more certain I was that this was the most likely scenario. I shared my thoughts with Jon and he gave me the "sure, if that makes you feel better go ahead and think that" look.

Although that look did not instill confidence, my own powers of denial were strong enough to ignore even that and get a somewhat restful night's sleep. And as is widely known, controlling one's mind is an extremely difficult, yet necessary exercise in remaining sane for anyone not lost in a sea of their own narcissism.

And speaking of sanity vs. narcissism, the next morning arrived with not only a meeting with Dominique and Officer Bachmann but also an email from my favorite nemesis, Clovis Cordoba Seville.

An email from Clovis is tough to take any time of day but before you've had your first cup of coffee it's intolerable. I had thought one good thing about investigating a murder in Switzerland would be a lack of Clovis.

A few years ago, Clovis worked at Marcel and managed to drive me insane on a daily basis. I thought when she left the company the pain would end but it was not to be. Apparently, Clovis has appointed herself as my personal Jiminy Cricket, sitting on my shoulder telling me what to do and reminding me constantly that I am far from perfect.

If I have a flaw – and let's face it, I might have one or two – proximity to Clovis is less than ideal. Largely because she has the ability to magnify any relatively minor blemish into the

Hindenburg and broadcast that negativity far and wide. I have indeed come to think of Clovis as my nemesis.

I gulped my near scalding coffee and began to read:

Oh Donna. I am beside myself! I had to learn through the grapevine that you are investigating a murder in Switzerland and you did not invite me to participate! I don't know how you expect to arrive at a satisfactory conclusion when the one person responsible for solving all of your prior murder cases was me!

At this point my temples began to throb.

I can just see you now, running around trying to wow the Swiss citizens by boasting of your absent talents and fabricated investigating skills – those lovely people really don't deserve your ineptness! And furthermore, you add insult to injury by inviting those two menopausal birdbrains along as your elite team.

Of course, the three of you have nothing better to do, and as you know, my time is exceptionally valuable. You must have assumed I wouldn't find the time to bail you out once again, and you would likely be right! But haven't I always managed to bail you out before, regardless of my extremely important and heavily packed schedule? How could you possibly forget that?

Oh, I can certainly see why you would not want to have me along.

My presence would make all those you have managed to bamboozle realize where the real detecting talent lies. They would instantly see you for the fraud that you have always been.

You really are an embarrassment to yourself, Donna. And I should warn you that you'd better not think you can invite me now because I would turn you down flat!

But oh, you know me, how can I turn a blind eye on you when you're about to create an international fiasco floundering about as you do! As much as you try my patience to my very soul you must admit I have always managed to be there to set things right, and I suppose this time will be no exception. Let's plan a call later today or tomorrow. We can decide then whether or not I have to fly out there, or if I can fix your mess from here! Email me to set a time for a call!

This was not good. One of my major fears was confirmed. I could not hide from Clovis no matter how far I roamed. And I sure didn't need her constant berating if I was going to make any headway on this investigation.

In fact, Clovis' email incensed me at so many levels they would be difficult to count. I was outraged for myself, and offended for my two trusty comrades, who were more valuable in an hour than Clovis was in her entire lifetime. I could think of only one solution. I responded to Clovis' email explaining that I did not have the appropriate equipment to make a transatlantic call.

There. I had responded politely – which was no easy task – and had rid myself of Clovis. Just as I was about finished patting myself on the back, my phone rang. Damn!

"Hello Clovis."

"Donna, how dumb do you think I am? Well, I guess that just shows how dumb you are! I know you wouldn't be off cavorting in another country without having the appropriate communication skills to reach key folks in the U.S."

Oh well, I thought it was worth taking a shot.

"How silly of me."

"You know, Donna, I would have taken offense if I didn't believe that you thought you were telling me the truth. But sadly, I know your level of tech knowledge is so limited that you probably didn't realize what you do have."

"Nice to talk to you too, Clovis," I managed through gritted teeth. "Now what do you want?"

"Well, Donna, I am prepared to take over this whole investigation so that you don't humiliate yourself any further. No, don't thank me. I can see that you've garnered the attention of some important and highly visible Swiss individuals and we can ill afford the risk of you and your continued tom foolery proving undeniably that all Americans are dimwitted."

"Gee, thanks Clovis, I was wondering how I was going to emerge from this with my reputation intact. I can always count on you, can't I?"

"I can only hope they don't already know of your reputation. If they do, it might be too late to salvage any semblance of our pride."

"Well, Clovis, as fun as this has been, I am late for an appointment…"

"No, Donna, don't go! I need to fill you in on my action plan. I will start my investigation stateside…"

Blah, blah, blah, I'd stopped listening after dimwitted.

"And then, I'll fly to Switzerland. I'm sure Dominique will have a luxury flat for me to use, and then…"

"Oh, wait, Clovis, you're breaking up…"

Good-bye!

I was sure I hadn't heard the last of her, but I had had about all I could take.

I walked back into the living room trying to assess the damage that Clovis had done to my psyche. The last thing I needed was for her to fly to Switzerland and insert herself into this complicated investigation. In a flash of brilliance I thought to block Clovis' number from my phone. No more texts or phone calls. I was, once again, patting myself on the back when Babs walked in.

"Donna, what's wrong?" Babs asked.

"You've heard from Clovis, haven't you?" Peg stated more than asked.

No words were necessary. Just the thought of Clovis blanketed the room with a malaise that couldn't be shaken. So, we gave up and allowed ourselves to succumb to the horror that Clovis always wrought.

It felt a lot like reading Stephen King. I had to give that up for my sanity as well.

Luckily, I had little time to ruminate on Clovis and her dark arts.

[Chapter 26]

Dominique and I lost no time in presenting ourselves at the station to meet with the polizei. We were greeted by Dominique's friend, Officer Bachmann, and he led us into a room with four other polizei sitting around a conference table.

Officer Bachmann made introductions all the way around and offered us coffee before starting the conversation. Knowing that police station coffee is notorious for its hideous flavor, we politely declined.

The gentleman across from Bachmann was clearly the senior officer in the room – he definitely wore the most distinguished uniform by far and had been introduced as Kantonspolizei-Kommandant Egger - so he began the meeting.

"Frau Gisin and Frau Leigh, we were extremely concerned to hear that, in addition to your involvement in a murder investigation, there might also be a dangerous stalker following the two of you."

"So, then you do believe that this is a stalker?" Dominique asked.

"We do, indeed," stated K-K Egger, "we can think of no other explanation based on the information you have given us."

Although we kind of expected that, hearing it confirmed really took the wind out of my sails. I could see that Dominique was taking the news just as hard.

"Now what?" I asked in my "no fooling around" voice.

"Since we know this individual has been following Frau Gisin and we can only deploy one officer to handle this concern, we will have him follow her. As you will not have a separate officer, Frau Leigh, we recommend that you either stick close to Frau Gisin or make absolutely sure that you go nowhere alone."

Both Dominique and I began to protest. She for not wanting a polizei escort and I for knowing I wouldn't be able to stick close enough often enough to be protected. But K-K Egger cut us both off.

"Ladies, I am confident that within a very short time, our officer will apprehend your stalker and bring her in for questioning. She will not be set free until we have a better understanding of her involvement and her intent. We are also hopeful that she will be able to give us more information about the murder. Assuming she is connected to the victim, and we are fairly confident that she must be, she could well be the lead that will - how do you Americans say — crack this case wide open."

And he continued.

"Frau Leigh, Officer Bachmann will give you some pointers on remaining safe in such a situation, just to be sure, but I cannot stress enough that you are to be with Frau Gisin or others, never alone. At least not until we have captured and interrogated the stalker."

On the way back to the flat in Dominique's car, with her assigned officer behind us in an unmarked polizei car - we discussed the new stalker protocol.

"You know, Donna, I never wanted a protection detail."

"I'm sure. But I do think it makes sense as a way to capture someone who's up to her eyeballs in this murder investigation. It's much harder to put all the pieces together when some of them are in Engelberg and some are in Pennsylvania."

"You make a good point. But I guess I am also feeling guilty that I will have protection and you will not."

"I appreciate that, Dominique. But I think if there is only one officer it does make sense that he protect you first and foremost. Not only because of your celebrity status, but also because we are sure the stalker is following you and only guessing that she's also after me."

"I do worry for your safety, Donna."

"Trust me, Dominique, I have read enough murder mysteries to know exactly what NOT to do in this type of a situation. You will not see me sneaking off to meet a stranger at midnight – alone. You will not see me question a person of interest without plenty of back up and until this women/stalker is caught you will not see me going or staying anywhere alone!"

"I know you say that now, Donna, but you have found yourself in potentially very dangerous situations in at least two of your three prior murder cases."

"Yes, there is that. But I can assure you that I did take precautions and there was potential for a whole lot more danger to which I didn't fall victim. And the main difference between then and now is, then I was cautious, now I will be paranoid! Now that danger has been confirmed I have officially marked this point in time as Code Red, and I will proceed accordingly!"

"I applaud your logical approach to this latest scare, but let me challenge your resolve. Jon and I are planning to go powder skiing at Laub tomorrow. Will you plan on joining us?"

"Very funny, Dominique. I know that Jon will be incredibly nervous to try to keep up with you on any slope, and especially in powder. I have a hard and fast rule – if it makes Jon nervous it will never get a chance to make me nervous. I think you know very well that I will not attempt to ski with you tomorrow."

"But then…" Dominique started, but I cut her off.

"Then I will accompany you to Laub and I will bring my posse along. The three of us will enjoy people watching and eating exceptional food with some lovely wine, in the lodge. So you see, I am prepared for any eventuality."

"OK, I surrender, you have got this whole thing figured out. But I must say, I would find it very boring to sit in the lodge and not get out on the snow."

"Yes, Dominique, that is clearly where you and I differ."

#####

"And for the rest of today?"

"I will be with Babs and Peg. I know that presents a whole other potential for danger, but it's one I'm used to."

At the flat I said my good-byes to Dominique who was off to another racing practice with Lyra. I was starting to forget our reason for being in Engelberg was Lyra and her racing career. It occurred to me that it wasn't fair to Lyra or her family. The time we were spending on everything but Lyra's racing was getting a bit ridiculous.

That said, I myself was rushing off with Babs and Peg to have lunch in Grindelwald and begin a search for Babs' ancestry.

We figured it was less likely that the stalker would follow me to Grindelwald, and if she did she would stand out a bit more. We left the car in the tourist lot just in case she knew what we were driving – it seemed safer on foot. Also, I was decidedly not alone so it was unlikely that she would try anything physical. At least that was our assessment.

The fact that Babs and Peg had already visited Grindelwald made our trip easier than I'd expected. They knew how to get there, where to park and where to grab a hearty snack.

They had also visited the city hall and had been able to narrow their search to three local families. After visiting the first two we learned enough to be fairly sure that the third family was related to Babs. On our way there Peg and I had some sage advise for Babs.

"We know this is super exciting," said Peg, "but try not to knock any part of their house or other property down."

Babs just rolled her eyes.

"You know, guys, I'm not just a walking wrecking ball!"

"Well," I began, "we know you never intend to be a walking wrecking ball, however…"

"Oh come on, give me a break. You know most of those times it ended up that I had actually done a good thing."

"Surprisingly, that is true," Peg concurred, "however, any one of those "happy accidents" could easily have caused severe bodily harm to yourself and others. You've just been lucky! And you can't keep counting on luck!"

"I disagree. I don't think it was luck at all. I think my instincts kicked in and guided me to take care of what had to be done!"

We were getting nowhere. Maybe it was time for some silent prayer!

At least we had yet to see a female who appeared to be stalking us. That was a plus. It would be difficult enough to keep control of Babs without a stalker causing her own kind of trouble.

[Chapter 27]

Luckily, Babs and Peg's knowledge of Grindelwald extended to public transport since our final and most promising family resided way across town from our current location.

As we boarded the bus I felt as though eyes were on me. And not just the "tourists who stand out in a foreign country" eyes, but somewhat sinister eyes.

I did my best to shake it off since I knew the odds were against us being followed all this way by the stalker, but I just couldn't shake myself back to normal.

"What's wrong?" Peg asked.

She knew me far too well to believe a deflecting response.

"Do you feel as though someone is watching us?"

"Now that you mention it, Donna."

"Come on guys! This is my big moment. Don't spoil it by imagining a stalker who may not even exist!"

"Gee Babs, thanks so much for your empathy and concern!"

"Come on, you know this must be in your head – heads."

At that moment, the bus lurched to the side and we began to fishtail. Suddenly Babs was less sure that Peg and I were imagining things. As we desperately tried to regain our equilibrium the fishtailing got worse. It took a second before we realized that a very corporate, very American looking blonde had moved to the front of the bus and was assaulting and overpowering our driver. Within seconds we smacked into a light pole. As soon as the bus stopped a blond woman pushed open the door and took off in a run.

Once outside the bus, we could see that the way in which it had hit the pole came very close to wiping the three of us out completely. We had dodged a huge bullet!

There was no longer any doubt. Our stalker had followed us and was intent on doing bodily harm.

The fact that she'd taken off so fast heading east helped us determine our next move. We were heading due west, so we felt the chances of her following us were fairly slim. Otherwise, we would have had no choice than to head to the police station and hope they would believe our crazy sounding tale. No, we would continue on with our mission, keep watch for anything suspicious and try to finish things quickly before heading back to the car and Engelberg. Once safely there we would most certainly stop at the police station to fill them in on our stalker's latest antics.

We thought about calling Jon or Dominique, but that would just serve to upset them as there was nothing they could have done. I was sure we'd get an earful from them but I felt it was still worth it.

As we approached the front door of the family we believed was most likely to be related to Babs, she suddenly took a deep breath.

"Guys, what if I wreck their house?"

"Just keep your hands to yourself and you'll be fine," Peg cautioned.

"Yeah Babs, we have your back," I added.

"You've just gotten yourself all worked up. Let us do the talking until you're feeling more yourself," Peg advised.

"Yeah, okay, let's do this!"

We knocked on the door. Within minutes we had been welcomed into the home of the Kohlers, Babs' Swiss relatives. They could not have been more gracious. They even shared the results of their own search into their U.S. relatives since a distant cousin had assured them that some of the family had emigrated to the U.S.

We were privileged to meet Herr Kohler or Oliver, Frau Kohler or Albina and their two sons, 15-year old Luca and 17-year old Elias.

Babs was beside herself with joy and excitement. Maybe I was kidding myself but I swore I saw a family resemblance. These lovely people insisted we join them for food and wine and that we stay as long as we could and still return to the flat in the daylight.

In my sophomoric mind I could not get over the fact that Babs was related to a family named Kohler. After all, Babs and her husband were the king and queen of DIY. I was sure they had installed many a Kohler product in their numerous remodeled houses.

After everything that had happened I was content to sit back with my own thoughts and let Babs and her relatives carry the conversation. I was in my own little world, until I heard a loud noise and several noises not quite as loud.

All conversation stopped. The two boys ran to the back of the house where the sounds had appeared to emanate from while the rest of us held our breath.

"There's a woman out there," said Luca, "why is she knocking over our garbage cans?"

"Let's find out," shouted Elias.

Babs, Peg and I all yelled to stop them. We quickly explained that it was likely this was our stalker. And she might be extremely dangerous.

As soon as we had finished, Oliver, Luca and Elias ran out of the house each holding a household item in preparation for needed defense. I was worried that a fire poker might not prove to be a strong enough match for whatever this villainous woman might be yielding.

How wrong I was. After less than 15 minutes, the Kohler men all returned to the house, with a woman we could only presume was our stalker in tow.

Holding her at bay with two kitchen knives and a fire poker, Herr Kohler phoned the local polizie. At our urging, he suggested they reach out to the Engelberg polizei before coming to collect their prisoner.

In the meantime, we all took it upon ourselves to interrogate our prisoner who was not inclined to talk.

Albina searched the stalker and confirmed that she was not holding any illegal weapons, but we knew that she was quite capable of creating dangerous problems with the thoughts in her head and her two hands.

Once the polizei arrived we urged them to grill the stalker – we couldn't even get a name and she was not carrying ID (this was getting to be a theme!) on the bus accident. We assured them it was she who had caused the bus to fishtail and ultimately collide with the light pole.

After the polizei took blondie away there was a collective sigh of relief. It was understood that the Grindalwald polizei would work with the Engelberg polizei to transfer and process her. It would be a while until we would hear anything about who she was and what she was up to.

Without fear of being stalked, we were able to relax a bit more and spend some quality time with the Kohler family. Babs was in her glory and it was amazing how many of the Kohler family seemed to share her mannerisms. It was almost comical.

After a few hours we took our leave with promises that Babs and the Kohlers would never lose touch. They even began to plan a Kohler visit to the U.S. All in all we had to agree that this had been a particularly successful day.

#####

When we arrived back at the flat we were greeted by Dominique and the Bryners in addition to Jon. We lost no time in filling them in on our way too exciting day.

"Yeah and we figure the stalker followed Donna and tried to kill her today because she knew that it would be more difficult to stop Dominique since she's so much younger and much more fit," Babs explained.

"No we did not figure that!" I hastened to add. And she calls herself my friend? What the hell?

Apparently, everyone found my response amusing. Everyone but me. After the laughter died down we spent a few minutes speculating on what could possibly be the stalker's story. Was she a relative of the victim looking for revenge? Or were she and the victim both hired by a third party?

As relieved as we all were that the stalker was behind bars, we were starting to wonder if this whole thing was much bigger than any of us had realized. But one thing I could say for all of us – we were card carrying optimists. So, we decided to celebrate the capture of our stalker by finally scheduling our wine tasting dinner.

We had been wanting to plan a special dinner to celebrate new family and friend connections as well as Lyra's success, and frankly because we all enjoy excellent food and wine. Since we didn't know what else would be coming down the road with this investigation, we felt this was the perfect time to enjoy a tasty diversion.

We got to work planning our menu. Actually, Jon and Dominique set up a time to plan our menu and the rest of us were happy to let them take the lead on this. This would also be a great opportunity to invite the Kohler family to join us.

Whoever came up with the idea for the dinner had perfect timing. It was just what we needed to get our minds off the unknown and very possibly dangerous stalking situation. Who knew if she acted alone or if a replacement would be forthcoming? But we couldn't think like that and stay sane. No, we would all focus on our special dinner while still looking over our shoulders at every turn.

We said our goodnights with happy thoughts and the hope that the coming days would give us the answers we so desperately sought.

[Chapter 28]

The next morning Jon and Dominique spent an exhilarating few hours skiing powder at Laub. Thankfully, the arrest of our stalker meant we were no longer under tight security restrictions, but Peg, Babs and I went along and spent our time drinking hot chocolate and people watching in the cozy ski lodge just the same. We still hadn't shaken the paranoia of having a stalker, who might well have reinforcements.

We weren't able to catch much of the powder skiing from our comfy seats in the restaurant Ritz at the foot of Laub. Although, we certainly enjoyed the trek through a snowy forest 1,000 feet above Engelberg. And the ride on the steep, old cable car to get us to that plateau was nothing short of spectacular – but it was really really steep!

What little we did see once there was like watching a Warren Miller film. Both Dominique and Jon skied in gracefully arced turns that looked like a ballet in all white. You'd think that constant white spray in their faces would be intolerable, but from their cheerful expressions we could tell they were having the time of their lives.

Afterward, we headed back to the flat while Dominique went on to another ski area for a training session with Lyra. Fortunately, Jon never ate lunch because the three of us were still stuffed from the hot chocolate and pastries.

Mid-afternoon Dominique arrived at the flat after spending several hours in training with Lyra. Naturally, Jon was anxious to get every detail, which delayed the planning of the wine dinner just a bit.

Dominique gave Jon a full download of the session practically minute by minute. My take-away was that Lyra's racing techniques were developing nicely, she showed great promise. But it took them about 20 minutes to get to that conclusion. To each his own I guess.

One thing in particular did get my attention. Dominique mentioned that as they started out Lyra had been feeling ungainly and unstable. She had complained to Dominique that she sometimes experienced these frustrating physical challenges. She just assumed that these episodes were a remnant of her early muscular issues.

Dominique assured her that pretty much everyone experiences those clunky, awkward days and she suggested that Lyra think of a song with a good solid beat that could always help her relax. Right away Lyra mentioned "Perfect Melody" by Jonas Blue and Julian Perretta.

Dominique then suggested that Lyra stand still and think of that song. After a few minutes she could see Lyra swaying to the music in her head so she told her to hang onto that music when she took her next run.

After a few runs Lyra was stunned at how quickly she was able to regain her balance and her stance while thinking of that song. Dominique suggested that Lyra could also get the actual music and listen to it while skiing, however, she did caution Lyra that listening to music is forbidden in competition. Then she would have to rely on the music in her head. Dominique had even showed her the video of her own sister, Michelle, when she got caught singing to her music in the start area at a World Cup race. Lyra could not stop laughing and it probably also helped to loosen her up.

"It was very cute to see how excited Lyra got about using a simple piece of music to help with her rhythm. That just shows what a serious athlete she is. What other millennial would not constantly be listening to music, whether or not it was helpful or hurtful to the task at hand?"

We had to agree it was unusual that Lyra had never thought of listening to music while skiing. There again, that could have been a result of her earlier malady and her need to be overly focused in order to overcome her challenges.

"Alright, enough about racing! Are you two getting this wine dinner planned or what?"

"I guess there is no doubt where Donna's interest lies."

I rolled my eyes.

"You can say that again, Dominique," Jon agreed, "Okay so, Dominique, it will be up to you to select the restaurant."

"No problem there. I can already tell you that Alpenclub will be my first choice. They are right in the middle of town, close to the monastery with a lovely little wine cellar for private celebrations. It will be ideal. Let me contact them to see if the wine cellar is free any time in the near future."

"Sounds incredible. Assuming we are able to get in on such short notice, are there any particular foods and wines that you would want to have included?"

"I absolutely love BALIN, a Swiss red wine from Ticino. It is amazing, especially with the favorite local dish, Älpermagronen or a good cheese fondue or Raclette, which I would suggest for one of the courses too. They will easily find a substitute for Donna with her lactose intolerance.

For white wine, we definitely should taste something from Lavaux and Wallis, a good 'Petite Arvine' is always something amazing."

"Dominique, we had no idea you'd be such a great resource for fine food and wine. It seems there's no end to your varied areas of expertise."

"Well, I certainly enjoy an evening of fine dining, Jon. That I will not deny. For years I thought I had no idea about wine. And then a good friend, and legendary wine taster, told me to just go with my gut. That was the moment when I learned to relax and just enjoy what I like.

"Now, if you want to have something traditional in a many course meal you might want to have a Raclette, as I mentioned earlier. Absolutely lovely is the chocolate mousse at Alpenclub which comes served from a traditional basket, a must if we eat there, and sadly requiring another substitution for poor Donna."

"It's something she's become used to after years of dealing with her lactose problems. And often, in the states, we find that these dinners are not terribly flexible in offering her alternatives. You would be surprised at how many times we have to skip these dinners or I have to go alone because there are so few dishes that Donna is able to eat."

"That should not be a problem here. I am certain Alpenclub will provide wonderful substitutions that will not make Donna ill. Especially since we are a relatively small group it will not tax their resources terribly."

"Donna will be thrilled to hear that!"

"To continue, the 'Nüsslisalat' is also pretty famous and would also go as an opener. We have a lot of Scandinavian people in Engelberg, also as cooks, so something a bit exotic from the north, maybe a fish course would be realistic too."

"Seriously? That's incredible! We recently sent our DNA in to have our ancestry confirmed. It turns out that Donna is mostly Swiss – which she knew – and secondly Norwegian – which she did not know at all. It really is a small world.

"I think we're off to an excellent start here, Dominique. I'd better get busy researching other wines to go with each dish. Especially if you're able to secure a date fairly soon."

"Now that I know more of Donna's ancestry, perhaps she should be the one selecting our food and wine for this dinner."

Jon just rolled his eyes.

#####

Dominique was able to confirm that there was an opening in the Alpenclub wine cellar at the end of that week so we were booked and ready to go.

Jon was thrilled and just a bit nervous that he would have time to research and purchase all of the selected wines. Naturally, we would avail ourselves of wine from the Alpenclub cellar whenever possible, but there were so many wines we

173

wanted to sample, and some would be more difficult to locate than others.

It was imperative that they make final decisions on each course so that Jon could locate the best wines to compliment each, and Dominique was particularly interested in considering wines from the amazing wine shop right next to Alpenclub which is owned by the famous Hess family.

I was just glad that Dominique and Jon had taken it upon themselves to handle all the planning. I knew with their combined knowledge this dinner would be exceptional. I also hoped that Dominique would be able to include her whole family in the dinner. I was most anxious to meet them given everything I'd heard and read.

I was glad that the wine dinner was finally booked since it was high time we checked in with Officer Bachmann to see what the polizei knew about our stalker.

#####

Dominique and I decided to head over to the station. We asked Officer Bachmann to join us for a short coffee break.

"Hoi Hermann, Donna and I are hoping you'll be able to join us for a quick break. As you can imagine, we are extremely curious about our stalker."

"I would be most happy to join you ladies, but I am sorry to say that I have very little to tell about your stalker."

At the closest café we found a table and quickly ordered from the offerings on the daily blackboard. Even knowing there wasn't much intel on our blonde interloper we were anxious to hear what little there was.

"So, Hermann, tell us what little you do know," Dominique started, ignoring the Swiss penchant for talking around a topic rather than being direct like their neighbors from the north, the Germans. In a murder investigation it is sometimes necessary to break the rules.

"Well, Dominique, we know that her name is Linda Badner and she is American. We have not been able to tie her to an exact location or a company. At this point, our thinking is that she may be in possession of a false identity which will make it far more difficult to get any accurate information."

"Shoot," I shouted, apparently a bit too loudly from the faces that turned toward me. "Now what?"

"Our research, based on what we found in searching the phone and credit cards that were at her hotel, would lead us to believe that Frau Badner had not existed prior to her flight to Switzerland. This tells us that we will have to change our research tactics to ones that have the ability to locate more covert operatives. Unfortunately, these searches tend to take quite a bit more time than our normal inquiries."

"Donna, do you think this kind of exploration might best be done directly from the U.S.?" Dominique asked.

"That's certainly possible, Dominique. I'm not sure who would know how to go about such a search though."

"Would it be worth a call to your friends in Utah, do you think?"

"It's worth a shot."

We resolved to call them at 5 pm our time, or 9 am Mountain time.

"Another thing," Hermann added, "We spoke to the Kohlers in Grindelwald."

I cringed.

"No need for concern, Frau Leigh, the Kohlers told us that finding their U.S. relative was the best and most exciting thing to happen to them in years. They cannot wait for their visit to the U.S. – or as they put it "their visit to the wild wild west."

"Well that's just great," I responded somewhat sarcastically, "Babs found her relatives, who are apparently her interchangeable doppelgangers. Just what we need in the U.S. – more Babs!"

I'm not at all sure why Dominique and Officer Bachmann found that so funny.

Upon departing Officer Bachmann cautioned us not to assume that we were completely out of danger just because this stalker had been apprehended.

"There is no way to know how deep this conspiracy goes and how many more people are involved. You need to take just as many precautions until all our questions have been answered to our satisfaction."

That certainly put a damper on things.

[Chapter 29]

Once on the call with Laura-Nicolas and Gerald we wasted no time in pleasantries.

"We're calling because…" that's as far as I got before Laura-Nicolas jumped in.

"Well, Donna, let me tell you what I've done'"

"What you've…"

"Don't worry, she'll tell you," Gerry piped in.

"I went online and did some research. I realize that with no job history, your victim will be difficult to pinpoint, so I researched businesses and work done in Pennsylvania. After that, I spoke to people either Gerry or I know to determine which would most likely have either a connection to Switzerland, skiing or something and even which would most likely be involved in undercover corporate intrigue and here's where I netted out: Chocolate – as you know, we have Hershey and Hershey competes with the best, and, of course, Switzerland is also known for chocolate."

I heard Dominique make a strangled sound. I was glad she chose to suppress her major disagreement with that statement so as not to get into a chocolate dispute with Laura-Nicolas and her love of all things Pennsylvania. And Laura-Nicolas went on.

"I also found Harley-Davidson motorcycles, and let's face it, everyone knows Harley - you either love them or hate them, and then there's all the pharmaceutical companies in Pennsylvania, and I know they are prevalent in Switzerland as well, and finally Yuengling Lager because I know that Germanic folks do love their beer."

"Wow, L-N, you've done an amazing job."

"Yeah, except for the chocolate…" Dominique began but I gave her a quick head shake – we'd have to have that discussion after the call.

"Thanks, well I'm not quite finished yet."

"Really?"

"Did you think she would be?" Gerry added.

"I'm dying to hear what else."

"With Gerry's help I've been able to identify connections to folks from each of these areas that would most likely be privy to any undercover corporate shenanigans. Some of these folks are no longer employed by the company in question – but are aware of the company's approach to competitive issues and some are still there and surprisingly willing to discuss competitive practices with folks they know. This will not be a short-term assignment – but I plan on having a list of any products that would create reason to be concerned about Swiss competitors."

"Holy cow, you are really something L-N!"

"She is an unstoppable force, no doubt about it" Gerry added.

"Well Laura-Nicolas I have a bit of a story to share with you."

I proceeded to fill the Völlmers in on Linda Badner and how she was caught stalking me. We agreed that having Linda's name might well help to home in on one specific industry.

Presumably she would have a work history record and finding Linda might lead us to Beau.

"The great part is that I've already identified the key people for inside information and they will certainly be able to tell me if a Linda Badner has ever been employed in their company. That should cut the interview time down by quite a lot and get you an answer much sooner," Laura-Nicolas said triumphantly, "Oh and we should definitely get her photo in the event that she is using an alias."

"Were you a detective in a past life?"

She was happiest when she was on a difficult and complicated mission and began to see a light at the end of the tunnel.

We thanked the Völlmers profusely and said our good-byes.

Dominique and I reviewed the call in astonishment. The Völlmers had taken it upon themselves to do a colossal amount of research for us. What would we have done without them?

We both agreed that Laura-Nicolas' tenaciousness would be an enormous help in finally solving this case. And there was that niggling feeling again. If nothing else, it was telling me that Laura-Nicolas was really onto something. I noticed that Dominique was looking a bit nonplussed.

"What's concerning you?"

"Well Donna, never in my life have I felt like the person who didn't try the hardest or contribute the most. But after listening to Laura-Nicolas and all the intel you and Tom have gained…"

"Join the club, Dominique. Everyone feels that way when they're around Laura-Nicolas. She is an absolute force of nature. But once you get used to it – you realize the benefits are well worth your feeling like a lazy slug."

"Yes, that's it – I feel like a lazy slug and this is new for me. Donna, do you really feel as though we are doing enough toward this investigation? After everything Laura-Nicolas has done."

"I get it, I totally get it. It's Laura-Nicolas syndrome. And just think how Gerry must feel. After all he's done to help – no one is in the Laura-Nicolas category! No one!"

Dominique nodded her head, but I could tell she was still feeling a bit disheartened. It would just take time.

"But it's really not just Laura-Nicolas."

"Yes, well Tom is an expert analyst, but remember, he had a physical piece of evidence to evaluate and years of experience doing just that. And as far as I'm concerned, thank you for giving me way more credit than I deserve. I will take my place in the slug category. I'm kind of getting used to it."

On the plus side, I was able to persuade Dominique to stay for dinner since Jon had volunteered to cook. Now why do I have the feeling that she wouldn't have been as anxious to accept if I'd told her I would be the chef du jour? Oh, I'm sure I'm mistaken. I think.

We enjoyed a lovely meal of shrimp risotto and some red wine, that Dominique and Jon agreed was perfect with the meal, and we regaled Jon, Babs and Peg with a recap of our conversation with the Völlmers.

"Wow, they've done so much to help with this investigation," Babs lamented, "I really feel like a stick in the mud."

"Now Babs,"

"No Donna, all I've done is sightsee, find my relatives and eat great food and wine. How have I helped at all?"

Laura-Nicolas syndrome again.

"Well Babs, I can genuinely say that finding your relatives when we did went a good way toward possibly saving my life from that stalker. You know if I had encountered her alone my chances might have been slim to none."

"That's a good point, Donna. And just think, if that stalker had tried to attack Dominique she would have had her butt kicked halfway across Switzerland. I would hate to have seen how she ended up after an encounter with Dominique."

"Hey, I might have kicked her butt too!"

"Oh yeah, sure, I'm sure that's what would have happened, Donna."

"Well then stop laughing! I mean it! You call yourselves friends. Apparently, it's true, 'no good deed shall go unpunished.' That's the last time I try to make any of you feel better about yourselves!"

The next morning Dominique stopped in at the flat before heading to the slopes to get Lyra ready for the following day's race.

"I heard from Hermann this morning. You know, Officer Bachmann. I was able to fill him in on the Völlmer's research and he was absolutely thrilled. Based on their interrogation of Linda Badner they were certain she had been a top level manager in a corporate position. The fact that the Völlmers will likely be able to find the exact company would be crucial to the investigation."

"Did he have any news to share with us?"

"Yes, but mostly news drawn on observation vs. fact. He did not believe that Badner had ever been an enforcer, but rather an interested party who likely had a stake in the success of her corporation. It is thought by the polizei that Badner was responsible for sending Beau to Switzerland and that she herself had subsequently been dispatched to try to obfuscate the trail so that it would not lead back to her company."

"I guess she wasn't counting on our tenacious crew here combined with the power of the Völlmer equation. Poor Frau Badner does not stand a chance. But I can't help wondering why she followed me into Grindelwald."

"That is still a mystery, Donna. She has not shared anything of substance with the polizei yet. But the more intel we get from our feet in the street in the U.S., the more likely she will begin to fill in the picture for us. Do you have any idea when we are likely to hear back from Laura-Nicolas?"

"You saw how fast she works. It could be later today or tomorrow. Of course, with each extra layer she has to work through she will be slowed down slightly."

"But I'm guessing she will not let anyone actually slow her down. Am I right?"

"Now you've got it. Slow for L-N is like warp speed for most anyone else."

Dominique and Jon both headed out to work with Lyra for her final training session before tomorrow's race.

That gave me time to spend with Babs and Peg. They would be welcoming the Kohlers to Engelberg and helping them check into their hotel for tomorrow night's wine tasting celebration.

We were expecting the Kohlers to arrive at 10 am so we had no time to lose in heading over to their hotel to meet them as they arrived. Once there, Babs wanted to do a quick inspection. Even though Dominique had recommended Hotel Bellevue Engelberg. Babs being Babs, she just had to give it her own seal of approval.

After a quick trot around the public facilities, Babs arrived back at the lobby just in time to see the Kohler's car pull up. We all helped them unload and there were hearty greetings all around. Once checked in, we asked the Kohlers how they would like to spend their first afternoon in Engelberg. They all agreed that watching Dominique work with Lyra would be top of their list.

I wasn't sure if that was the best idea. Partly because I knew there were only certain spots where we would be able to observe the training, and partly because these people were all related to Babs. They couldn't all be like Babs, could they? Not to mention that there would be some skiing involved and we hadn't exactly set the slopes on fire with our questionable expertise.

It turned out that the Kohlers had thought to bring their ski gear – so only Babs and Peg, would have to rent equipment in order to ski to a spot that would enable us to best watch the training.

We grabbed a quick lunch at the hotel. The Kohlers decided to hang back at the restaurant while the rest of us headed over to the slopes for equipment.

#####

It wasn't even close to pretty, but Babs and Peg skated, sledded, walked, belly slid, and side slipped their way to our destination. I fared quite a bit better, but was hardly feeling confident. We made it just moments before the Kohlers arrived all looking like a crew of ski instructors. I was sure Babs must be secretly glad they had not witnessed her farcical attempt at skiing.

We all breathed in the fresh mountain air, waiting for something to happen. We waved to Dominique, Lyra and Jon. At the moment it appeared that there was more talking than skiing going on. But then, we were watching a training session not an actual race.

After a few moments, Lyra moved away from Dominique and Jon and pushed off to ski down the slope. Dominique and Jon were not far behind her and occasionally we could see Dominique pass Lyra and make a hand gesture to her. Lyra would just nod slightly. I didn't know about the others, but this seemed riveting to me. I was intrigued by their graceful ballet of skis, poles and occasional hand gestures and was trying to think of what music this snow gliding dance would best fit.

After a bit our entertainment moved temporarily out of view. With a cursory look to Babs I could see the wheels turning in her head. She wanted every second of her relatives' visit to be gripping, but that just wasn't reality unless you were at Disneyworld, and even then those long lines…

[Chapter 30]

I could see Babs' eyes darting around for something to grab her relatives' attention and keep them from being bored. She suggested we all do a little skiing ourselves. After all, we all had the gear.

"Wait, what?"

"Come on, Donna, you saw how much better we were doing today!"

Was she kidding? What I saw was a miracle they hadn't killed themselves. This could not happen!

My brain was going 1,000 miles a minute. I didn't think there was a slope nearby that I could feel comfortable skiing – and I knew I skied a whole hell of a lot better than Babs and Peg. Let's face it, at least I skied. What they did – I have no idea what you'd call it!

I was certain the Kohlers would likely be fine anywhere, since they had some notably serious equipment and had looked damn good coming down the hill, after all, they did live in Switzerland. I was getting more nervous by the second as I realized Babs was eying a nearby slope, an extremely difficult slope.

"Uh, Babs, maybe this is not…"

"Nonsense Donna. There's no handle this slope to your right."

"Actually Babs,"

"There, that's settled, let's go!"

The Kohlers all took off in a mad dash leaving Peg, Babs and me to head over and try to make our way down. Within 10 seconds the Kohlers were out of sight and the three of us were left to fend for ourselves.

This was new for me because I had never tackled an exceedingly difficult slope without Jon by my side. Having him ski with me was essential because he knew my skills better than I knew them myself. If I found a particularly daunting section of the slope and was concerned it was beyond my skills, Jon could give me an honest assessment of my capabilities. That generally bolstered my confidence enough for me to get down with one or two helpful tips. In this way I had skied my way down many black diamond slopes over the years. I was never able to beat Jon, but I had always made it down – so far.

Without Jon's counsel I stuck to blue or green (that's in U.S. ski lingo) and only the easiest of blacks – and ones that I'd done many times.

But that was me, and Babs and Peg had done none of that. In fact, I was fairly certain they'd never struggled down anything more difficult than a green run – and I mean really struggled. This run was not that.

I could see after the first few turns that this was going to be quite a challenge for me. I did not hold any hope for my two companions. And what's worse, they didn't even know enough to know they couldn't possibly handle this slope. I was in a panic over how I would get the three of us down in one piece.

In retrospect, getting down was the easy part. The hard part was picking up the detritus left in their wake. What could I possibly mean by that? I'll tell you.

Babs took three snowplow turns and fell at the top of a very steep plateau. And then she began to slide. The further she slid the more her equipment broke loose in a freefall of its own. Have you ever heard of the snowball effect?

Babs had become the lead snowball, followed by her skis and then her poles. I think I counted 6 victims hit directly by Babs and 4 more by her skis. Her poles, smaller and lighter, flew between the legs of two very fast skiers. I had never before equated skiing with parasailing – but that's kind of how it looked.

And as for Peg. She made it through 5 turns before her body turned into a human cannonball hurtling through mostly air – she only touched down on the snow a half dozen times.

All told, between the two there were over a dozen bodies lying prone or in heaps over the top two-thirds of the slope. The carnage was everywhere! Each heat seeking missile, Babs and then Peg splatted to a stop within about 30 yards of each other.

Within minutes the slopes were covered with ski patrollers and rescue toboggans. It was like nothing I'd ever seen before.

I, myself, had been utilizing a method taught to me at Gray Rocks Snow Eagle ski school, north of Montreal. I skied what I felt I could – and side slipped down the rest. And when I say skied – I took it at my own pace and did not employ much in the way of excessive speed.

I skied around the casualties and their rescue folks until I got to Babs and her patroller.

"Is she okay?"

"We'll know better when we get her down to first aid."

"I'm fine – did you see me hit that woman in the Bogner suit? Man, she went flying. I bet that glamorous fashion suit never saw speeds like that before!"

"Hey Babs, maybe don't talk."

"Ma'am. Would you like me to send a sled for you?" asked Babs' patroller.

"Are you looking at me? Is he looking at me? NO, I don't need a sled, why would you even say that?" I asked utterly offended, "I'm getting down of my own volition I'll thank you to notice!"

"Your volition is not looking so good today. But whatever you say."

I harumphed my way around the rest of the casualties until I reached Peg and her toboggan.

"Are you okay, Peg?"

"Yes, I'm just mortified. Why did Babs…"

"Do you honestly think I know?"

"Ma'am…" started Pegs' patroller.

"No I do NOT need a toboggan, and I will thank you not to say one more word about it." What is it with these people? Don't they recognize a semi-competent skier when they see one?

"Whatever you say, jerry, I mean Ma'am."

"And while you're at it, cool it with the Ma'am! And my name's not Jerry either!"

"Yes, Ma' – I mean."

"Just forget it."

I pushed off and continued my ski and side slip trek down the hill. I hadn't realized there was quite a bit more to this slope than where Babs and Peg had landed. As I methodically made my way down I was able to see every toboggan on the hill pass me as though they were just mocking me.

Babs and Peg were whisked off to first aid with the rest of the casualties, so I was left to explain our plight to the Kohlers and wait in anticipation of what would surely be their derision. Much to my surprise, Herr Kohler just laughed. That sounds much like a ski trip we made 4 years ago. There were some British skiers on the slopes and they kept falling in front of us or on top of us. You would be amazed at how many toboggans were required to get us all down to safety.

I should have known. After all, they were related to Babs. And frankly, I've seen enough fallout from British skiers that I could have guessed that outcome.

After all was said and done there were no serious injuries. That was a huge relief! The Kohlers and I collected the two culprits and prepared to head out. The senior manager for Mt. Titlis walked us to the parking lot.

"Well, Frau Leigh, I would just like to let you know that we will welcome your group to ski at Andermatt at any time in the future," he stated with a serious face, but a slight twinkle in his eye.

"But this is…Oh, I get it." My face turned what I assumed was a lovely shade of bright red. We couldn't get out of there fast enough.

Luckily, tomorrow's race would be held at Andermatt so we wouldn't have to face him, even on foot, for at least a few days.

[Chapter 31]

We grabbed a quick lunch at Restaurant Espen before heading back to our flat where we gave the Kohlers a quick tour before embarking on our afternoon plans. Since we'd already attempted the skiing thing we felt an afternoon of sightseeing might be safer. Of course, with Peg and Babs was anything really safe?

Luca and Elias were pushing for extreme sports and cave hunting. After the morning we'd had, I felt we'd experienced enough death defying adventure so I suggested we head over to the Benedictine monastery, despite the slight letdown the boys tried so hard to hide. Having been there once already, we knew they would perk up once they saw all that the monastery had to offer. At this point my number one goal was to keep everyone out of the hospital and on their feet. And that would be no small task all things considered.

Once there we found various aspects that peaked our individual interests so we went our separate ways to explore. All except Peg, Babs and me that is. I was not about to let those two out of my sight for an instant. We could ill afford another incident in Engelberg. God forbid we would end up being escorted out of the city. I shuddered to think of the humiliation that would cause everyone involved. I doubted I'd ever be able to look Dominique in the eye again – although the fact that she allowed us free reign in Engelberg was a true testament to her belief that everyone deserves a second chance. Or a fifth or seventh – whatever.

The afternoon touring was a rousing success and we all returned back to our flat in good spirits – and with a great sigh of relief. The Kohlers insisted on cooking a dinner for the rest of us, including the Bryners. We would have to make it an early night as Lyra had to be in prime form for the important race tomorrow morning.

One good thing about the day's misadventures, we got some genuine belly laughs when we retold, and relived, the tale. Apparently even the Kohlers had no idea of exactly what had transpired since they had successfully maneuvered the slope that brought the three of us to our knees – in some cases literally.

At first we shared details grudgingly, and watched Dominique and Jon turn a bit ashen. Once we assured them there were no serious injuries – not even any broken bones or sprains – truly a miracle - and we saw the hilarity that ensued by sharing just a few underplayed tidbits, we began to loosen up and let the actual facts fly. In truth, considering that we were three former advertising folks, we took exaggeration to the cliff but kept it just shy of tumbling over. It was truly a performance worthy of the Comedy Club.

Once the laughter died down, it occurred to me that together we had shared something invaluable. Partaking in a lovely meal prepared by the Kohlers had undoubtedly helped to form a most welcome bond, but sharing an unbridled belly laugh was the glue that pulled people into a tight and unbreakable attachment.

After all our earlier angst over the skiing mishap, we ended the day feeling happier than we could have imagined. Our fear of being humiliated by being laughed at melted once we realized that what we'd done was pretty damned funny. Embarrassment turned to euphoria when we allowed ourselves to join in the fun and laugh at ourselves.

The fact that no one in our audience took their humor to a meanspirited, mocking level made all the difference. Of course, the three of us lost no time in mocking each other.

"You looked ridiculous heading downhill on that sled with your head bobbing all around."

"Yeah, well watching you try to sideslip around all the other skiers made me almost wet my pants."

"You were looking at the ski patroller as if he was about to propose."

"The hell I was, I saw you watching that patroller's butt, don't think I missed that little drool coming out of your mouth!"

As we began to get more raucous, the rest of the group helped to settle us down. I guess there was just a bit of residual angst after all, but we seemed to be able to finally get it out of our systems and laugh at the ridiculousness of the whole thing.

The Kohlers were surprised to learn that we good naturedly blamed the whole fiasco on them. Had Babs not been so eager to impress her newfound relatives with her skiing proficiency none of this would have happened.

"Well," Babs lamented, "I was doing so well the other day. I thought I was getting to the point of advanced intermediate or even expert."

"Babs, you never got out of a snowplow."

And that's when the laughter started all over again!

#####

The next morning came earlier than expected. We had to be in top form in order to support Lyra in this race. And then, tonight would be our extra special wine dinner. This was going to be a long day!

At breakfast we discussed the importance of this junior race. Jon pointed out that Dominique had encouraged us to attend this specific race at Andermatt because some of the World Cup Athletes would attend, which was momentous for such a race. They would be able to attend due to having a short break in their schedule, but would be tired and not at their absolute top form. At least that would be true of the athletes who focused on one or two disciplines – for Dominique's sister, who skis all the races there is no such break. The exhaustion of the World Cup athletes would give the more junior racers a slight advantage – and in ski racing that can be just the edge you need.

In her first run Lyra would be at something of a disadvantage because the World Cup racers would be starting early. But, if Lyra did well in this first run and made it into the top 30, she would be one of the first out of the gate for the second run when the gates would be set up differently.

We knew that Lyra's bib was number 84 which could mean she would be lagging behind if either the World Cup athletes pushed themselves to the max or if the disadvantage of being 84th out of the gate significantly impacted her performance. So we would all be holding our breath as we watched.

Luckily, on this course, we would not have to be on skis to be spectators – since the staff at Andermatt might not be thrilled to see Babs anywhere near the t-bar.

After breakfast, Jon, Babs, Peg and I all piled into the car that Dominique had loaned us to head over to Andermatt. We would meet the Bryners, the Kohlers and Dominique on the mountain near race time.

The parking lot was nearly full when we arrived. We hoped the rest of the crew had made it there already. And within a few minutes we were relieved to see that they had.

There was just enough time to get suggestions on best viewing from Dominique and to wish Lyra well. I was so impressed that she didn't even look nervous. But then I realized that the top athletes often have to be able to hide their nerves – I thought maybe that would bode well for Lyra as she progressed. I actually thought Dominique looked a bit nervous, but being the mentor was quite different from being the trainee.

Dominique always looked in command of her nerves from the videos I had seen of her racing. With Lyra, Dominique had poured her heart and soul into prepping this young talent and as much as she had a huge amount of confidence in her pupil, confidence isn't control. I could see just how much this race meant to Dominique by the way she kept pulling on her glove. We would all be relieved when this race was over.

I could see this was an important race just by the enormous crowd that was forming. Jon filled me in that this was not the norm for a race at this level, but was probably drawing such a huge crowd due to the World Cup racers that would be attending. Now I was really starting to get nervous. I could tell Babs and Peg were feeling the same because they were both extremely fidgety. What scared me a bit was that I could see Babs looking around for a place to inspect. Her inspections did not typically end well for anyone in the near vicinity. I had to distract both of them.

"Hey Babs, didn't the Kohlers say they knew someone who was racing?"

"I don't remember hearing that."

"Well, maybe they just follow one of these racers, you'd better find out so we know who is rooting for whom." I was trying to think on my feet but even I could hear how lame I was sounding.

"I guess I can always ask them." Thankfully, I'd bought us some time – maybe.

Babs shuffled off to grill the Kohlers and Peg lost no time in calling me on my BS.

"Don't think I don't know what you did there."

"I can't think what you mean."

"That's fine, it's just as well you've sent her on a wild goose chase. It will keep us all safer."

Sometimes the end does justify the means.

As the time for the first run grew closer we all migrated over to get in the best viewing position. The excitement in the crowd was growing exponentially and when the first racer left the gate the air was charged with electricity.

It was so exciting I barely noticed how long I had been standing in the freezing cold. It was mesmerizing or I'd have been lobbying for a hot chocolate break. When Lyra finally appeared at the starting gate I was pretty sure I was holding my breath. Or maybe I just forgot to breath. The suspense was killing me.

I watched her graceful form fairly float through each gate and honestly couldn't tell if her speed was any less than those who'd raced before her. She looked amazing.

As fast as she went her race seemed to take an eternity – I know, holding my breath didn't help. When she finally hit the finish line our group went totally wild. I think we made the most noise yet. And then when we saw that she had finished 28th we somehow got even louder. We knew that 28th was exceptionally good because the previous night Dominique and Jon had given us a bit of a primer on what the different starting numbers meant.

This was such an incredible experience. Lyra would be one of the earlier racers in the next run and that would absolutely give her a bit of an advantage.

The time between the first and second runs could not pass quickly enough. We decided to try and find a hot beverage and warm up a bit, but it appeared that all the other spectators had the same idea. If nothing else we would have to find a restroom.

It was actually a good thing that there was a fair amount of time between runs. It took pretty much the entire time but we were able to get all of our needs satisfied and get back into our viewing spot.

The second run was no less exciting than the first. If possible, Lyra looked even sleeker and faster this time. And to our great joy and amazement, she finished 22nd. This was undeniably an important day in Lyra's career and we were there to share it with her in person. Tonight's wine dinner would truly be a huge celebration!

#####

Much to both my sadness and relief, Peg spent the afternoon confirming plans for both she and Babs to leave in a few days. Our lovely little – not so little – flat would feel so empty without them. But also without them I might not get the ulcer I was beginning to feel was inevitable.

Babs, on the other hand, spent the afternoon with her newfound family. Walking by you would never know that they hadn't spent their whole lives together. I had never seen Babs look so euphoric. She was really in her glory.

I, on the other hand, spent the better part of the afternoon helping Jon verify that everything he and Dominique had requested for our special dinner, had been obtainable. And after some extensive checking, it appeared as though all systems were go. So it was time to get showered and dressed for our big night.

[Chapter 32]

We arrived at Alpenclub, which was located in the middle of town close to the monastery, precisely on time. Dominique and her family were there within minutes. We were thrilled to meet her family, all champion athletes within their own right. Undeniably an extremely impressive household.

Dominique made introductions all around. We got to meet her parents, and her brother and his wife. We were disappointed that her sister Michelle was unable to join us for this dinner, but the fact that she was on the World Cup tour was certainly an excusable absence. Besides, we knew we would have the opportunity of not only meeting Michelle, but possibly even watching her race in St. Moritz.

It was immediately evident that this was a close-knit family. So comfortable together, and so proud of each other. And yet, so open and welcoming to all of us. We were all aware of Dominique and Michelle's Olympic triumphs, they would have been hard to miss. But her brother was also a national asset having been fifth in the Streif – the most infamous race in the World Cup – two times. And the fact that all three of these national treasures all heralded from the same immediate family was beyond comprehension.

In keeping with their typical humble demeaner, their Mom put an end to the sports talk with but a simple statement.

"Yes, it's wonderful that our children have found their passion and have been fortunate enough to excel in their chosen areas. But for a mother, it is extremely challenging to

201

find the time to get together as a family. In fact, in 25 years we have only managed to get the whole family together for one night each year, Christmas Eve."

Wow, that really was a challenge. Especially when you could see how much they all enjoyed being together.

As we entered Alpenclub, we were greeted by an exceptionally gracious and very lovely hostess, Lena, who would be our guide throughout the evening. She was so clearly appreciative that we had chosen Alpenclub as our venue and she assured us our evening would be unforgettable.

She also took the time to assure me that all the courses were prepared fresh, so they were able to find dairy substitutes for my dishes in order to accommodate my lactose intolerance. That was a huge relief. It is rare that restaurants are able to accommodate my special needs in the states. I typically find that I am eating less than I ordered because they remove certain items without bothering to replace them or they remove flavorful ingredients without finding a substitute – yet they don't charge less money when I'm eating only a portion of a meal, and that portion is without flavor.

Our hostess explained that their strong Scandinavian connection dictated that they provide a selection of excellent dishes without gluten or lactose. It was not considered to be problematic. Here was yet another area where the U.S. could learn a thing or two.

Lena then walked us to the lovely little wine cellar which would be the venue for our private wine tasting celebration.

As we removed our coats, we were offered a glass of Swiss Eiswein, although more of a German delicacy, it is sometimes featured in Switzerland and typically after the meal. Jon had made a special request, that we start the celebration with this wonderful wine – he just didn't want to wait! Weingut Elfenhof Schwiez is well known for its incredible fruity sweetness featuring both stone and tropical fruits. This wine was paired with cheese (and no, there's no non-dairy substitute for that – even the Swiss Gruyère was too much of a risk) and nuts and was served as we moved about chatting with everyone in our party. Once seated, it would be a bit difficult to converse with everyone in such a large group.

As I was enjoying the wine and some nuts, a platter of delectable fried vegetables arrived for all of us to ensure that my experience was every bit as delightful as that of the lactose eating folks. I could really get used to this!

What a lovely way to be welcomed, of course, Lyra and her siblings would be drinking sparkling non-alcoholic cider for the duration of the evening. The folks running our dinner even thought to provide a side offering of Crémant d'Alsace Cuveé Prestige for those of us who are not accustomed to enjoying sweet wines at the onset of the meal.

Naturally, I had to try both. Not being a huge fan of sweet wines, I was most pleasantly surprised by the Eiswein. It embodied a natural tasting sweetness that kept it from having that harsh, almost bubble gum taste of wines that have added sugar in their process. And the Crémant was amazing – I could have stayed there drinking both options all night. But, moving on to our first course proved a treat not to be missed. One thing was certain, I was glad I wouldn't be the one driving even the short distance home!

As I moved around the room, I managed to catch words and phrases within the various conversations. Heading over to Babs and the Kohlers, I realized that the Kohlers were regaling Dominique's family with our Engelberg mountain mishap from earlier in the day. I stood a moment to hear if they were mocking and humiliating their newfound relative, Babs, for causing such chaos on the ski run. I couldn't help but smile when I perceived that they were doing just the opposite.

Instead of mocking and embarrassing Babs, they were making her out to be some sort of skiing stunt person who'd been brought in to make all the other skiers laugh. I just shook my head. If I'd had any doubt that the Kohlers were Babs' relatives, that story cemented their connection like nothing else.

And true to form, Babs just stood there smiling. She always walked away from these incidents with the carriage of a victor. Luckily, the Gisins were a kind and supportive audience and never questioned how a person who manages to knock down virtually everyone else on a ski slope could possibly be considered an entertainer. Although she was ultimately able to enjoy a hearty laugh with the rest of us, Dominique's Mom took a moment to ensure that there had been no real injuries.

It registered in that moment that I would really miss Babs and Peg when they returned to the states in a few days time.

#####

The first course did not disappoint. This was the one area where Dominique and Jon had disagreed. Jon had argued that a pasta course should come first before the meat course, but Dominique had held firm that this particular pasta course she had chosen would make you not want to eat the beef, but rather have another dish of the same pasta. Naturally, having tried all of these specialties, Dominique prevailed, so our first course was Lummelbraten, a beef, butter, garlic, onions, carrots and celery in a mustard, red and white wine sauce. The meat was lightly fried and deglazed with wine and then boiled for a short period. It was lovely when served with an equally exquisite Gantenbein Pinot Noir replete with wood notes and fruit that combined for a heavenly roasted aroma.

There was far less conversation as we all savored each bite while the chef appeared to explain the dish and the sommelier came next to enlighten us on the delightful wine we were drinking. It was difficult to believe that any of the other courses could possibly match the one we were eating. I laugh to think of the folks that feel the need to climb high mountains when true adventure can be had at a fine restaurant with exceptional food and drink.

While resting after the first course and awaiting the second, the conversation turned toward the Gisin family, their athletic prowess - and the lack of athletic prowess displayed by one notable member.

We were to learn some things about the whole Gisin family, but particularly about Dominique. It seems as though, before any thought of ski racing or the Olympics came into the picture, her parents had some reservations about Dominique truly feeling comfortable in their uber-athletic family.

They loved their little girl but, had become distressingly aware that she exhibited challenges in regards to certain athletic abilities, i.e. she could not catch – or get out of the way – of a flying object. She was evidently lacking in the ability to sense an object coming at her – even if forewarned. Her parents could not see a way for her to overcome such a basic shortfall in order to excel in any kind of athletics. You're either athletic or you aren't – she wasn't. Right?

Having been the victim of a few misplaced light poles and a sliding door screen or two myself – I was particularly sensitive to her 'challenges,' and the mocking that was inevitable from those close to me.

We learned a new word that day. Her family referred to Dominique as a "jerry," i.e. she was prone to fumble. Wait, that word sounded vaguely familiar – had I heard it before? I'm sure not.

We were regaled with stories of Dominique's penchant for always standing in the wrong place and getting hit with anything from a rain spout of water to an out of bounds tennis ball, for watching car keys drop into a sewer drain by missing even the simplest of catches. We heard of her penchant for getting hit with odd objects (like a 'fresh out of the oven' croissant in the 5th arrondissement) in famous places all around Europe and we all shared in the laughter, especially Dominique.

Her Mom was quick to assure us that, while they took her 'jerry-like' challenges in stride and acknowledged her role as the family comedian, they were secretly concerned about her ability to feel like a real part of this exceptionally athletic, overachieving family.

Both parents tried their best to underplay the athletic successes of Dominique's parents and siblings without giving short shrift to their other children. A challenging balancing act to be sure since her sister, younger by eight years, was skiing Laub by the age of five – and doing her best to escape her father's watchful eye. Her brother was undeniably the natural athlete of the family.

The happy and surprising culmination of their concerns was the fact that Dominique proved to be so incredibly good on skis. No one would have guessed that. And Dominique assured us that, even before her racing success, she never felt inferior or picked on. A true triumph in parenting.

"One thing I can say for sure, I was always the first one to laugh at my own 'jerry-ness.' And if I'm honest, I still provide my family with much entertainment as I continue to get smacked in the head with flying objects – sometimes even while on the snow. If they need cheering up, they only have to yell 'here, catch, Dominique' and then everyone explodes into laughter."

As Dominque and her family finished their entertaining revelations, the second course was served. And, as the second course was making its rounds, Dominique's friend, Officer Bachmann made an appearance. We had invited him to join us for the wine tasting, but with the murder investigation still very much underway, he was unable to commit. We had made it clear he would be welcome to join us during any stage of the evening.

As Officer Bachmann made his way around the table for introductions, Dominique and I glanced knowingly at each other. This would be an excellent time to get an update over some lovely food and wine. We did not need to talk to each other – we knew instinctively how to grill our polizei friend.

"We are so pleased that you are able to join us, Hermann."

"Yes, we know how hard you must be working to tie this whole investigation up into a nice, neat little package."

"That is precisely correct. We have been working non-stop to get to the bottom of this puzzling mystery. It will be wonderful to get a much needed break this evening. Perhaps afterward my brain will process the information better and a solution will come to me."

"Hermann, you know that Donna and I are more than willing to help you sort through the details to try to make sense of them."

"I do not doubt that, Dominique, but I will not ruin a perfectly lovely evening by talking about a most unsettling murder. It would not be appropriate dinner conversation, and it would certainly not provide me with the break that I seriously need."

Dominique and I just looked at each other. Well shoot, we couldn't argue with his logic. Before either of us had a chance to speak up, everyone else chimed in to make it clear that they would relish a discussion of murder during their special dinner.

"Okay, okay. Let's just agree to this. If we get further through the dinner and I am feeling renewed and ambitious about investigating once again, I will share what new information I am at liberty to share. That is the best I can promise you."

And we'd take it!

The second course arrived just as we were starting to feel slightly peckish again. So as not to weigh us down, this course was chosen for its lightness. Fresh pike with a cream sauce (lemon sauce for me) was delectable and crisp. It was served with an exquisite 2018 Gantenbein Chardonnay which introduced peach, citrus, fresh melon and pineapple on the nose along with a stony-mineral impression. Both clear and complex with a fine toast aroma the pairing was indescribable and just right for the moment.

After a brief respite where we all enjoyed ourselves eating and drinking what seemed like perfection, Dominique and I exchanged meaningful glances. Then we each covertly checked on Officer Bachmann to determine if now would be the time. After several seconds Dominique looked at me with a barely perceptible head shake, now was not the time. I shrugged my agreement.

Not surprisingly, the conversation turned to cooking and Officer Bachmann shared several of his grandma's (or Grosi as he called her) recipes with an eager audience. This could be why I spaced out until the third course was nearly under our noses. As much as I love to eat, there has yet to be a recipe that will get my undivided attention. This was a good opportunity for me to remind myself of what we'd learned so far in the investigation, and what we had yet to learn. I wanted to be prepared for anything our officer friend was willing to share.

As I looked around the room I caught a glance at Lyra. Clearly, she too was bored by talk of recipes, but was there something else concerning her? She should be absolutely euphoric about her successful race, but in looking at her, that didn't seem to be the case. I glanced at Dominique, who was seated next to Lyra and caught her eye. I motioned toward Lyra with my head.

I could see from the glimmer in Dominique's eye that she had caught my meaning. She turned and whispered to Lyra. For a few minutes, they whispered back and forth and then a faint smile appeared on Lyra's face, and then there was a small but genuine laugh. Clearly, Dominique had been able to assuage her concerns.

[Chapter 33]

The third course was Älpermagronen, the Engelberg specialty served with applemousse. Put simply, it was Swiss Alpine macaroni and cheese with not only pasta but potatoes, cheese (of course), cream and onions sautéed in the caramelized onions. My substitute course did not disappoint. They left out the cheese and substituted cream with Coconut milk. I'm sure my fellow diners felt sorry for me and I was secretly glad they wouldn't ask for a taste. This dish was amazing, dairy or no dairy. Needless to say with this course being a must, both Dominique and Jon had agreed we (they really) would forego the raclette course for fear of a drastic cheese overload – even for Switzerland this would have been a bit much.

The Älpermagronen was paired with a 2015 Cantina Kopp von der Crone Visini Balin from Ticino. It had a vivid red, oak-derived, smoky-bacon nose with ripe plum. This was a beautifully elegant Merlot with a small amount of the Arinarnoa varietal.

Thankfully, the fifth course was a salad. Nüsslisalat to be exact, featuring corn salad or Lambs Lettuce with bacon and eggs. Lovely and light it was paired with a Weingut Rienan Sauvignon Blanc from Basel. This was a strong yellow in color with an extremely complex bouquet of mineral and savory aromas including mace and white pepper followed by fresh apple fruit, citrus and some vanilla.

Sauvignon Blanc is my favorite wine. I tend to favor wines from the Marlborough region of New Zealand, but this Swiss offering was a most welcome surprise. Knowing my preference, Dominique sneaked a bottle of her favorite, Rimapere, for me to try at a later date.

The salad course was succulent and as light as air. The wine selected was a perfect complement. It was nothing short of delectable. After the third course we'd all been making noises to demonstrate that we couldn't possibly finish the meal even though we knew Dominique had asked for very small portions, we'd all had enough. But now, after our Nüsslisalat we were eager to move on to the next course.

And the next course was cheese. Although this was one course where there could be no close substitution I was treated to a small bowl of fresh fruit – and for me – there was nothing better. The others ate a selection of cheeses from the legendary cheesemaker, Willi Schmid. Willi's cheeses are not at all like the "holey Swiss cheese" that every American knows so well.

The cheeses were paired with the Marie-Thérèse Chappaz 2017 Petit Arvine Grain Noble from Valais which is considered the best sweet wine in Switzerland. Citrus peel, ripe light stone fruit, stone fruit like apricot and light flowers on the nose. Extremely intense and supple on the palate, while balancing acidity and minerality. It worked quite well with my fruit course.

It was during this course that our friend, Officer Bachmann decided he was ready to enlighten us. I think he was feeling sorry for me because I had to forego the wonderful cheese course so he decided to distract me with news of the investigation. Odd things can prompt human behavior, but I was not about to look this gift horse in the cheese-less mouth.

"So, Dominique and Donna, tell me what you have learned most recently."

"Well, Hermann, as you know, Donna and I had that Zoom call with the Völlmers and they were going to attempt to narrow down the industry where the victim and the stalker may have been employed, possibly under the table. We were planning on checking up with them later in the week to see if they have made any progress."

"Then I may be able to help them home in on a short list of industries based on our research with Basel's sister city of Miami Beach, Florida."

We were all ears.

"The folks in Miami Beach were able to zero in on two industries in which Linda Badner has worked, under her real name of Louise Bonita. This was a far more difficult task than usual and we were puzzled as to why. It turns out that Frau Badner has always been involved in corporate espionage and has therefore been able to maintain a low profile within every company where she has worked. Her job description also indicates that she could well have been somehow involved with our victim, since he seemed willing to take on any job, no matter how dirty or despicable."

"Don't hold back Officer Bachmann. Once you share this information we can pass it along to the Völlmers so they can work more quickly."

"Yes, well, we now know that Frau Badner has spent several years working in the Life Sciences & Medical Technology industry. And with her knowledge of that industry she was a perfect fit to move into the world of pharmaceutical science."

Bells and whistles were ringing in my head. The pieces of the puzzle were starting to fit into place. Hadn't I read somewhere that Beau had been selling bogus pharmaceuticals? We know pharma is a huge industry in Philadelphia, as well as where Will is employed in Switzerland. Had Beau been targeting Will? Clearly, this was a huge breakthrough, but there was a lot we still needed to know.

And then it was time for dessert!

Since Dominique had strongly recommended Alpenclub's chocolate mousse and hot chocolate, that was the dessert for our tasting. And because we had given them plenty of notice, they were able to make a mousse and hot chocolate for me with Coconut milk, so I was able to share this extra special treat with the group. It did not disappoint!

Not everyone had the fortitude to handle both the mousse and the hot chocolate – so some paired up and shared these treats. And all of this was served with yet another Eiswein, Schmitt Sohne Ice Wine, with similar properties to the cocktail party wine, but subtle differences such as strong aromas reminiscent of tropical fruit. It was voluminous with rich essences on the palate.

Very little talking occurred during the dessert course, but there was quite a bit of groaning. At first I wasn't certain if they were caused by pain or euphoria – ultimately it was euphoria.

As I began to recover from my chocolate high (and yes, milk chocolate does contain milk, so I'm safer with dark chocolate thanks to the influence of those Scandinavian chefs) Officer Bachmann's words jumped around in my brain. If nothing else, we would have to phone the Völlmers right away, both to double check the findings as well as save them from any extra work in evaluating their whole list of possible industries. I would email them when I got back to the flat and request a call for early afternoon tomorrow. It suddenly occurred to me that my cousin, Will, was in the pharmaceutical industry. It was remiss of us not to have asked him about his work in all this time.

"So, Will, now that the subject of pharmaceuticals has come up, it occurs to me that we don't know very much about the work you are doing. Can you tell us a little about it?"

"Well, Donna, I am currently working on an anti-aging drug that will ameliorate many of the challenges of aging."

"Can I put my order in now?"

"I'll take a dozen of whatever that is."

"You've been holding out on us!"

"Well, not intentionally, I assure you," Will laughed, "this drug is able to keep inflammation at bay and inflammation constitutes so many challenges for folks as they age. And for me, the best benefit was that, after going through an enormous amount of paperwork and approvals, this experimental drug

215

focused on aging was able to help Lyra with her extremely rare condition. There would never have been funding for a drug to help her otherwise – her condition is that rare."

"That's amazing!"

"It is because the majority of rare conditions will never receive pharmaceutical help. The industry is so focused on ROI and the return on R&D for a rare condition is virtually non-existent. It was only through a fluke and the fact that I, Lyra's father, was the researcher on this particular drug… And without all necessary approvals my career would have been over and the drug would have been unobtainable. We were so very fortunate."

"Oh yes, that's right, we had heard that. And it is still simply amazing that, even with the help of the drug, she was able to overcome her challenges enough to be a solid competitor in ski racing. Will, you are really a hero!"

"Oh no, I am hardly a hero."

"Yes, Dad, you are my hero," Lyra insisted, "you have made everything possible for me."

There was not a dry eye in the house.

After dessert and once the waterworks were under control, there was a feeling of content, combined with a bit of sadness that this incredible meal had come to an end. Jon was beaming from ear to ear and I knew it was more than just the wine he had drunk, but the fact that he was able to cross another must off his bucket list. So far he had 1/seen Lyra train and ski, 2/he had himself skied with his Olympic idol and now he had tasted an array of 'Swiss' wines that few people we know have been able to try. He was a happy guy!

I took advantage of a quiet moment to question Dominique on her earlier conversation with Lyra.

"What could possibly make her unhappy today?"

"Do you remember one of the later racers, a young girl named Etta who fell in the first run?"

I nodded.

"Lyra said that she injured her knee in that fall. And Lyra is concerned it could end her racing career. I thought this would be the time to share all the sordid details of my own story of injuries from falls, my numerous surgeries and the work it took to get back into prime racing shape. I never shared all of that with her earlier so as not to frighten her unnecessarily."

"And that is a powerful story, indeed. But now I can't help wondering, what on earth in that story made her laugh?"

"Two things. Her initial laugh was when I shared the part about putting Topfen curd cheese on my knee to stop the swelling. If you remember, Donna, I recommended to Jon that he put this cheese on your knee when you injured your, MCL, PCL and meniscus while trying to avoid hitting a couple of novice skiers a few years ago."

"I'll never forget that. At first we thought you were kidding, but it was amazing how well it worked to reduce the swelling. And, I have to say, we were the laughing stock at a whole bunch of dinner parties while trying to explain my healing process. We had to prove it was true by Googling injured European athletes using the cheese - on several

217

occasions. I'm so glad you were there to help Lyra through her fears right then and there."

"Yes, that was fortunate."

"So, what else made her laugh?"

"When we spoke of the injured skier, Lyra asked me if I thought she had a 'spirit animal' that would help her in her recovery. It was such an intuitive comment, so I asked if she had one. We both laughed when Lyra acknowledged that her 'spirit' animal was a peregrine falcon. That was a surprise, so many of us choose feline 'spirit' animals for their speed. But Lyra set me straight, she said peregrine falcons live in Switzerland and are the fastest animals in the world. She also asked me 'and sometimes, don't you just feel as though you're flying?' This kid has a good head on her shoulders!"

And her concern for her fellow racer is also an excellent sign. Any racer out for just themselves is truly not destined for greatness – at least not in the hearts of the people. Lyra has a good heart and that will upset her at times, but ultimately it will serve her well."

And there it was. I was getting another lesson in being a top-level athlete. I may have intuited some of these things, but hearing them directly from Dominique made them so much more real.

Luckily the flat was nearby so we thanked our hosts and all made our way back to get a good night's sleep. We agreed to all meet at our flat the following morning. The Kohlers wanted to prepare a big Swiss breakfast for us before leaving for home. I couldn't image how I would be able to eat again in just a few short hours. Spoiler alert – I managed.

As I was heading to bed I took a minor detour to check my email. Our dog sitters wanted to let us know that Frank and Ellie were having a wonderful 'vacation,' but we would be in big trouble when we got home! Now I was beaming. It's always great to get news of "the kids" and to hear that they're enjoying themselves. A sudden feeling of exhaustion along with a slight case of homesickness had me crawling under the covers in record time.

At eight the next morning our kitchen was filled with the noise of a major breakfast production. All four Kohlers were gliding about preparing various dishes for us. I was genuinely impressed with their ability to function at such a high level after the evening we'd had. I guess that was another way that Babs and her cousins were similar. No matter how long and arduous things might become, Babs was always ready to jump in and take on another task – no matter how formidable.

At the risk of sounding like a cookbook, the kitchen was filled with Zopf (braided white bread), a variety of Swiss cheeses and cheese fondue (chocolate fondue for me – god help me!), Kleine Schweizer quiches, Pastetli (meat pie), Buttergipfeli (croissant-like pastry with less butter) and Birchermüesli. And last but not least Zimtsterne Cinnamon cookies. Don't worry, even with all the dairy there was still plenty for me to eat – and thoroughly enjoy.

Once again, we ate until groans were heard all around. Then it was time to bid the Kohlers safe travels. It was a sad moment for all of us – especially Babs. There were tears and promises of meeting again soon and staying in touch via video phone, etc.

Once things settled down, Dominique and I took a moment to plan an agenda for our upcoming call with the Völlmers. Once our gameplan was established, we all went our separate ways, Babs with her new relatives, Peg and I sightseeing, Jon and Dominique skiing with and training Lyra.

[Chapter 34]

The next morning, we were all exhausted and agreed that we'd give ourselves a rest break. Dominique and I were mentally planning for our call with the Völlmers. The intel we'd received from Officer Bachmann last night would really help to narrow their search. At this point, we weren't even worried about comparing and combining notes since Dominique and I had been in lock step regarding this whole investigation.

We ate a light lunch at the flat and cleaned up quickly in order to, once again, review our notes and get ready for our call later that afternoon.

"So, Laura-Nicolas and Gerry, let me tell you…" That's as far as I got before Gerry chimed in.

"Just let her give you an update."

"But our latest update…" Too late, it was already 'go' time.

"Dominique and Donna, our interviews have narrowed things down quite a bit."

I tried one more time to jump in and save them valuable time and energy – to no avail.

"We now know that Linda Badner is Louise Bonita. Louise spent years in corporate espionage in the pharmaceutical industry. And, as you may recall, Beau had some nefarious dealings of his own in that industry. We have concluded that the connection between Switzerland and Pennsylvania is pharmaceutical, and we believe that Louise and Beau were working undercover together and in all likelihood, not terribly

221

ethically. We know you are aware that Will Bryner is a researcher in pharma so we've concluded that this is the sweet spot in this investigation."

"Unbelievable!"

"Elementary, actually." Now she was quoting Sherlock Holmes.

"But how, I mean when…"

"How we got this is past history. Now, you need to find out what part of Will's research has created fear in a pharmaceutical company in Pennsylvania. That shouldn't be too hard, and it should lead to exactly what Beau and Louise were attempting to do."

Our call with the Völlmers was short and sweet. In a nutshell, they had garnered everything the Swiss police had learned from their Miami Beach connection and tied it up in a nice, neat little bow.

Dominique and I were blown away by the Völlmers' precision, accuracy and speed. I would have to talk to them about opening a detective agency. Their talent for investigating was downright stunning. They were right, Will had to be the target, but of what and why?

As I pondered our conversations both with the Völlmers and Officer Bachmann, one thought kept rising to the top. We happened to be around when a tragic death occurred, so we jumped in to help find the solution. The search took us on an international tour from Switzerland to Pennsylvania and back. Yet, the final conclusion was right under our very noses. My own, newly found cousin Will was the key to everything. Have I mentioned it's a small world?

Dominique and I spent an hour or two speculating on how and why Will was the key to this whole thing. Did the aging drug he was researching present a huge competitive concern for a pharmaceutical brand in Pennsylvania? That didn't seem to make sense. I mean even if there was a competitive brand in the states, the drug wasn't even through the research phase and was nowhere near ready to begin marketing. These steps could take years. I could see them wanting to conduct competitive espionage to determine the status and efficacy of the drug – but physically harming the researcher – that just didn't make sense. And in a ski area no less. Granted, he does ski and he has a house near Titlis, but it still seemed quite a stretch.

It was clear that we'd have to take a close look at the pharmaceutical companies in Pennsylvania that were researching drugs on aging. And our next logical step would be to interview Will in great detail. Perhaps there was something he already knew that could help us understand the final pieces to this puzzle.

Since there was no time like the present, we decided to bring 'take out' to the Bryners for dinner that night. While the rest of the crew was having fun, Dominique and I would take Will aside and interview him on everything and anything that could be relevant to the investigation.

Once we finished with our Think Tank, we filled Jon, Babs and Peg in on our plans for the evening. They could entertain the rest of the Bryners while Dominique and I met with Will.

Jon smiled his approval – apparently, we were still headed in the right direction. Part of me felt vindicated, while another part felt his smile was just a little too smug. By the look on Dominique's face I could see she was with me on this.

Babs and Peg offered to order and pick up the pizzas so the rest of us could get organized for that evening. They decided to get the pizza from Bierlialp. I didn't think that could get them into trouble. They left with promises of meeting us at the Bryner's. My mouth was watering as I saw them head out the door.

An hour and a half later, Dominique, Jon and I were on our way to the Bryner's house. They greeted us with bottles of Davoser Craft Beer, I stuck to Guiness myself. We were truly getting immersed in the Swiss culture. They also showed us the various chocolates they'd be serving for dessert. I did my best to convince them that chocolate and beer would be a great compliment. They were not convinced.

We'd been there a full 45 minutes and still no sign of Babs and Peg. I tried calling and texting – but nothing. I had just about gotten to the point where I was contemplating a search party when the smell of hot pizza caught my attention.

"What took you so long?"

"Relax, Donna. You can see for yourself we're both here and unharmed."

"You didn't answer the question, what took you so long?"

"We just took our time, it's not like we're in any kind of a great rush."

"Do I look like I was born yesterday?"

"Well, if you must know, we wanted to savor the experience, just as we've wanted to savor each experience here in Engelberg."

"And precisely what does "savoring experience" in a pizza restaurant in Engelberg entail?"

"Geez, I don't remember you being this pushy before. Okay, fine. We took the time to chat with the owners – they were excited that we had chosen their restaurant on this, our first trip to Switzerland. Babs was encouraged by their warmth and friendliness and she happened to mention that a lifelong dream had been to make a "professional" Italian pizza."

It was getting really hot in here.

"And?"

"And they insisted she try in their kitchen."

Things were starting to go black.

"Yeah, and it was more fun than I could have imagined. I was like a pro rolling out the dough. I flung that dough in the air a couple of times and caught it just like you see in the movies. It was awesome."

I started to feel a bit calmer – more fool me.

"But then, after she did an incredible job selecting all of the toppings and spacing them perfectly on the pizza, she did one more thing."

"I don't know why I thought the pros throw the pizza in the air one more time before placing it in the oven."

Now I was hyperventilating.

"Yeah, so this time, the pizza hit the ceiling and stuck there."

"NO!"

"Yes! And then within minutes it peeled itself off the ceiling and landed – splat – in the middle of the array of toppings. I mean, onions covered with ceiling dust landed in the sausage and the mushrooms. The pepperoni made it all the way over to the sauce itself as well as the mozzarella. I think you can imagine the rest."

"And how are you back here at all and not in a cell down at the station?"

"The owners weren't happy."

"I think that's probably an understatement."

"They said if we cleaned everything up and threw away Babs' pizza and all of the tainted toppings we would be free to go."

"Unbelievable."

"Yeah, and Donna," Babs said with a grin and a blush, "we got all the pizza for free as long as we promised not to go back."

I was speechless. There stood Babs, grinning like the cat that swallowed the canary, obviously thinking she had once again emerged a hero. I was still speechless.

"Oh yeah and Donna, the pizza crust landed on the chef's head so he quit on the spot. We might want to try to talk him into rethinking that. I'm sure they'd hate to lose such a talented pizza chef over such a minor incident."

"Minor?" I only hoped that said it all because I had nothing left to give. Maybe saying good-bye to this duo in a few days would not be the worst thing. I could only pray that they would not change their minds and decide to extend their stay.

I was suddenly aware of a great deal of hilarity around me. It took a few seconds to realize they were reliving the great pizza disaster and cracking everyone up. Was I the only one who'd been horrified by their antics? Had I lost my sense of humor? Since I was still struggling with the ability to speak, I decided to shut up and watch the show unfolding around me.

I had to admit, after a few more minutes and a couple of pieces of pizza I was starting to see the humor. Let's face it, humor is infectious!

After we finished with the pizza, it was time to get busy interviewing Will about his research. After sharing a great belly laugh, everyone decided to sit and listen as we began our discussion. We were all so entrenched in this murder investigation, no one wanted to chance missing an important clue. So, Will began to share his story.

"I was hired to try to find a drug to help fight inflammation in the elderly. You may be thinking there are already several drugs on the market for that purpose, and you'd be right. But the owners of Mornovato, my employers, believed there was a way to make a drug that would improve mobility in the elderly far more than anything existing today. Once they enlightened me on the specifics of their hypothesis, I was hooked. I had seen my grandparents and both Greta's parents and mine struggle with near debilitating discomfort as they aged and nothing they took would miraculously enable them to move around effortlessly, as they had in their youth. When they were in excruciating pain and took pain medication, the impact on their stomachs was a whole other kind of pain."

We all understood, as we had seen the effects of inflammation in our elderly family members. A drug of this type was sorely needed (sorry, bad pun).

"Once I began searching for the excipients that would make such a drug viable, I became even more immersed in our plight. And the continued contact I had with folks suffering from inflammation made me more and more determined. As you know, these drugs often take years to formulate and then more years to test and get approved. I worked tirelessly day after day to make this dream come to fruition. Simultaneously, I watched as my beautiful young daughter became less and less mobile from a disease or condition that remained undiagnosed. It was painful beyond belief that I couldn't just drop what I was doing to find a cure for my own child."

I fought so hard to keep the tears in, but when I saw the faces and tears all around the room it was a lost cause. So much for my Swiss stoicism.

"One day Greta had to take our two youngest to the doctor so she asked me to take Lyra to the lab that day. I was leery of bringing a child into such a potentially dangerous environment, but I had little choice. I sat Lyra in the corner with a coloring book and crayons and went back to my work. A sudden noise pulled me out of my heavy focus. Lyra had gotten bored and walked over to the table holding the newly formulated pills. I caught her just in time before she ingested a pill that had not been meant for anyone under the age of 65. It was a close call.

"That's when I started thinking. The more I had watched Lyra as she struggled to move around, the more I realized the similarity to the elderly patients I had been researching. I had also noticed that those taking our drug had significantly better mobility than those taking any of the other drugs already on the market. Yes, this drug was indicated for inflammation in the elderly, but why couldn't this drug work for Lyra if it seemed to help older folks in our testing?

"I realized if that were the case we would have to get approval to use it as an Off-Label drug since Lyra's condition was too rare to attempt a full drug repurposing, that would never yield an ROI for Mornovado. I thought I was really onto something, and that filled us all with hope.

"And, as it turned out, with another year of work to finish testing and get approvals we were able to try the drug on Lyra. You know the remaining part, miraculously she was healed and the rest, as they say, is history. Each day she became better and better. One day, when she had been running for the first time, Lyra confessed her dream of becoming a racer. Greta and I worried that, all things considered, this would be too much of a stretch for her poor, fragile body. But we were determined to give her all the inspiration and motivation we could – we never tried to crush her dreams.

"We hoped we'd made the right decision, praying she would find another, less strenuous interest when the time came. As you know, that turned out to be unnecessary. Our Lyra is nothing short of a hero the way she has worked and trained and we could not be more proud of her."

We took a moment to dry our tears before getting to the interrogation part of the evening.

"Now Will, can you think of a company in the U.S., particularly in Pennsylvania, that might have a problem with the work you've been doing?"

"That's just it. There are several companies that already feature a drug for inflammation. There are even drugs in varied strengths for the increasing levels of inflammation. But I have never yet heard of a drug that is successfully doing anything beyond what has already been done. And that has been sadly lacking.

"There's really been no publicity about Lyra's rare condition and her remarkable recovery doesn't seem to have broached even the outer most boundaries of a small ski community here in Switzerland. It's really only the locals that are aware of Lyra's miraculous recovery."

All I could think was that dear Will was shockingly naïve of the workings of the pharmaceutical industry.

[Chapter 35]

Today was a bit sad. It was time for us to drive Babs and Peg to the train station so they could get back to the Zurich airport. I could already tell I was really going to miss them. Not only were they interesting companions, their comical misadventures served to pull attention away from any one of the stupid things I might do. Selfish? Yes, and I freely admit it.

As we waved goody-bye to our dear friends I thought I heard someone calling my name. I didn't think there were a whole lot of Donnas living around here. And suddenly I knew. I think I started to black out when I clearly heard…

"Oh for god sake, Donna, get over here and help me with my luggage."

Could I be dreaming? No such luck. Jon gave me a sympathetic look and we both turned around to see Clovis. A petit and somewhat emaciated looking blonde with aggressively frizzy hair and a designer outfit that swam on her – there stood Clovis Cordoba Seville – my nemesis.

"Here, just grab these two bags, Donna. Jon, you take these three. That way I can carry my handbag unencumbered. I'm glad you were at least thoughtful enough to meet me at the train station. You've been ghosting me for the past several days and I can't imagine why."

"Oh, well, my phone is missing." Unfortunately, it chose that moment to ring. Curses! Babs and Peg wanted to say their final good-bye.

"Right Donna. I take no offense. You probably did think your phone was missing. So typically you!"

"Now let's get these bags into the car and get me over to the flat so I can get settled in."

"Oh, Clovis, there just isn't room enough in the flat. It's awfully small." I was going to hell for sure.

"Fine. Then take me to the most exclusive hotel in Engelberg. I'm sure the police will reimburse my expenses once I've solved this murder for them."

We drove Clovis to the Kempinski Palace and waited until she checked in. When the bell-hop started to load her many bags onto a gurney, Jon and I attempted to slip away.

"Don't go anywhere yet. I want a quick debriefing once I get to my room. And Donna, why don't you see if you can have some refreshments sent up to my room while I'm directing the bell-hop with my luggage. At least try to be useful."

Damn! How would the hotel staff feel if I ordered a crème pie and shoved it into her face? They might not be thrilled today – but give them a few days with Princess Pestiferous and they would be paying me to do it!

Once alone in the lobby, Jon and I discussed this latest dilemma. We came to the mutual agreement that meeting in Clovis' hotel room would be the only way to avoid having her come to the flat. So, once again, we found ourselves bending to her will.

One thing Jon and I also agreed upon, we would not be sharing the details of this murder investigation – at least not any more than was already public knowledge. The real trick would be trying to avoid her over the course of the next few days. We had made a serious breakthrough talking to Will and we felt the conclusion to this investigation would be reached quite soon – without Clovis' interference!

After over an hour with Clovis we were able to extricate ourselves and make our way back to the flat. I phoned Dominique immediately to fill her in on our latest stumbling block.

"Thanks for the heads up, Donna, but I am not overly worried about this Clovis woman. We are already so close to the answers we seek, I cannot really see how she could get in our way."

"Prepare to be dumbstruck, Dominique."

I could hear her laughing quietly as we said good-bye. I genuinely hoped Dominique would not get a front seat at the Clovis Circus, but even as I thought it, I realized how hopeless it was.

That night we had all agreed to dine out once again. Dominique chose one of her favorites, and the food, décor and overall ambiance did not disappoint. We had given everyone a heads up about oversharing information so the conversation was deliberately and expertly directed away from the investigation. As soon as Clovis began her interrogation, Will set the tone for the whole dinner.

"Frau Seville, we would never insult a welcome visitor with discussion of anything as sordid as a murder investigation over a delightful meal."

I could see Clovis visibly deflate, but that did not deter her for long. She proceeded to regale us all with stories of her own travels through Switzerland. And Clovis was no dummy, so her descriptive narrative rang true with even the native Swiss. At one point, Dominique leaned over and whispered to me.

"I am not seeing the malevolence or the narcissism you describe in Clovis, Donna. And I am a bit shocked. It is not like you to be judgmental and your intuition is normally spot on. What is it about Clovis that brings this side out in you?"

"Just wait." I hated to think that Dominique would think less of me for being petty and small minded. That really did sting. I had only a moment to wait.

As we finished our scrumptious apple strudel and Torta di Pane Ticinese, the chef and owner came out to greet us and answer any questions we might have. Dominique took the lead.

"As usual, my friend, this has been an absolutely…" That's as far as she got. And then there was Clovis.

"So glad you chose to stop by our table. I can give you a detailed synopsis of the problems with my main course and my dessert. The rest of the dishes were more passable, but could still use a bit of help."

I could see the look on the Chef's face, and it matched the look on Dominique's face. It was something like extreme shock and anger mixed with incredulity and a certain purplish shade of red. Good old Clovis.

"Well, yes, let me tell you that I took top level cooking classes during three of my extended stays in Switzerland. I suggest you let me treat you to a cooking class while I'm still in the country – I could up your game by quite a bit. In fact, I am single handedly responsible for saving a handful of Swiss/German restaurants in the U.S. They were just not doing things correctly – but I soon remedied that. Frankly, I'm not here a moment too soon – I am certain I will be able to save your restaurant as well!"

At this point, I really had to hold back the laughter threatening to overtake me. I did not want to add insult to injury. When Clovis headed to the ladies' room I took the opportunity to assure both the Chef and Dominique that the meal had been nothing short of superb. I think it helped a little. At least the Chef was able to return to the kitchen. I then turned to Dominique.

"Do you…"

"Yes, yes, I see now."

#####

The next morning Dominique and I headed over to the police station. We wanted to share our theory with Officer Bachmann and anyone else who would listen. We waited for about 15 minutes until our group gathered in a conference room.

We agreed that Dominique would take the lead and fill the officers in on our thoughts and concerns about Will. Our details were clearly outlined in a leave behind outline. We were so organized.

"So, gentlemen…"

Before she got any further, we heard a clatter outside the room and much to our amazement the doors burst open revealing Clovis in all her glory. She charged right in saying...

"Don't trouble yourselves girls, I'll take it from here."

Dominique looked at me and I just shrugged. We had dropped her off at her luxury hotel the preceding evening with nary a word of our intended visit to the station this morning. And yet, here she was, in all of her snarky and narcissistic glory.

"I have prepared a brief slide show." And then she bellowed "where's the damn projector I requested?" The officer from the front desk came running in with projector in hand looking as though he was being chased by a tiger.

Once set up, the slide show was nothing more than a "I'm Clovis, look how fabulous I am" presentation designed to illustrate her overall brilliance, but, in particular, her investigating brilliance. She had photos of herself at several crime scenes and with several U.S. police looking as though she was in charge. It was amazing what photoshop could do these days. I knew for a fact that none of this was real, but I remained mute. Not for fear of upsetting the lunatic making the presentation, but more because I had not thought there was anything Clovis could do that would shock me. I was wrong.

At about the 15 minute mark, the feeling in the room shifted. Once her spectators realized that Clovis was not supplying information of any interest or help in the investigation their patience, and with it their courtesy, disappeared rapidly. Officer Bachmann was the first to speak.

"Excuse me Frau, we have not gathered in this conference room for the purpose of seeing a slide show of your life. We have actual work to do and for that reason I will have to ask you to take your slides and depart – immediately."

"Oh, but Officer, I thought you understood my importance in very many murder cases. I would imagine you would be thrilled that I inconvenienced myself to fly over here in order to enable you to close this current case. And I will certainly expect you to reimburse my expenses. I am certain Donna must have explained how critical I am in solving cases. Did she not?"

"She did not. And we have no time for such self-indulgent nonsense."

Wow, that was awesome! In all my years suffering through Clovis attacks I have never seen anyone put the petite tyrant so thoroughly in her place. Why had I never said that to her? I didn't even care that, as the front desk officer was silently escorting (dragging) her out of the room, she found the ability to twist her head all the way around and look at me with daggers of death shooting from her eyes. Yes, I knew there'd be a price – but it was so worth it!

Once the pint sized despot had been handily dispatched, we were finally able to get down to business so Dominique started where she'd left off.

She explained that we are of a firm belief that everything relating to the murder revolves around Will and his work in pharmaceutical. She shared every clue that brought us to that conclusion, and then went on to speculate that we believe Will must have been the intended victim, but we were left with three questions, 1/Why would a pharmaceutical company want to kill Will?, 2/Why would they choose to dispense with him at a Swiss ski area?, and 3/What pharmaceutical company would benefit by Will's demise.

The group was most appreciative of our work. While they themselves had been thinking the key connection could be a pharmaceutical company because of Beau and Linda's (or Louise's) backgrounds, they had not yet tied Will into the equation, and that was clearly the cornerstone that would enable the pieces to start falling into place.

"We still have Frau Badner (aka Louise Bonita) in custody for entering the country with a false passport but, as yet, she has refused to speak of anything related to the case, and she has not admitted to knowing our victim. Whether or not she speaks, she will do jail time, but the more details we uncover the more likely she will be to break down, admit her duplicity and fill in the remaining facts.

"Of course we interviewed Herr Bryner quite early on in the case, but once he was eliminated as a suspect we never considered his having any involvement again – even after we started to suspect that the pharmaceutical industry was the key, our focus was on the U.S. and Pennsylvania in particular. We didn't link him with the circumstances we were evaluating.

"Nor did we until Will shared his career journey with us the other night at dinner. As he spoke both Dominique and I started to connect all the dots. I could see we were in sync just by looking at the pensive expression on her face."

We said our good-byes and humbly took our praise.

"Oh, one other thing Frau Leigh. Our victim, Beau Jones was on your flight over to Zurich, and most likely shared the same train to Engelberg."

I was dumbstruck.

"You know what that means, Dominique? Peg and Babs were right all along."

"Well, isn't that something?"

Driving back to the flat, Dominique and I were finally feeling as though we'd made a significant contribution to this investigation.

"I have to admit, Donna. I was beginning to think this might be the first case you were not able to solve. And, if that were true, I would feel as though I had let you down."

"Actually, Dominique, this has been one of the more logical cases with which I've been involved. Most times we stumble around blindly until the murderer feels backed into a corner and eventually lashes out and confesses, kind of at the same time. At least in this case, I feel as though we've both been instrumental in helping gather solid leads and building on them with solid research."

"Well, Donna, there is one thing we know for certain in this case."

"What's that?"

"This murderer won't be confessing."

[Chapter 36]

I had a bad feeling when we pulled up to the flat.

"Donna, what's troubling you?"

"I'm sensing a dark cloud about to descend on me."

And then there was Clovis. As though she'd been laying in wait. I had barely gotten out of the car when she launched into her vitriolic diatribe.

"And you call yourself a friend, and you said they would cover all my expenses! You practically begged me to fly here and get you out of yet another mess. I will never forgive you for your role in this! My patience has finally worn thin, you leave me no choice but to drop you as a friend once and for all! I do not know how you will function without my help, you always flounder without my help! But that is no longer my concern!"

I looked over at Dominique and saw tears and that was it! We both burst into peals of uncontrollable laughter. The more we laughed, the more the miniature martinet shrieked like a screaming howler monkey, thus making us laugh even harder. I think it was the stress relief we both needed. It cleared our brains, hell, it cleared our sinuses.

Sensing our laughter was not about to end, and in all her righteous glory, Clovis stormed off and left us to stumble, still cackling, into the flat.

At some point during all the hilarity, it dawned on us that Clovis had stormed off. It took me a minute, but once I realized, I sobered instantly.

"Oh god, that's gonna come back to bite me!" But it turns out, I was mistaken. Clovis' anger kept her away from us for almost two full days. How had I not realized this before? All I had to do was piss her off and she'd leave me be? And yes, I knew our next meeting would be 'the return of the screaming howler monkey,' but to get such a break would be well worth that price. Besides, when we were together I was never bereft of a solid slew of incoming insults, so all in all I was ahead of the game!

We had planned a quick call with the Völlmers for after lunch. Our mission was to focus their interviews even more and add the details of Will's research to the equation.

And once again, the Völlmers had beat us to the punch.

"Okay so Donna," began Laura-Nicolas, "we've already started to narrow our search down to companies that are focused on inflammation, but we have focused our covert inquiries into companies that are planning their market expansion into the area of inflammation."

"Well, guys, that's wonderful, but market expansion, is this something that is extremely well hidden and closely guarded?"

"It is. And that's why our connections are so vital to this mission. We have been able to uncover secrets that we would never have been able to expose without them. And we wouldn't have known any of these folks if we hadn't come in contact with them over the years that we worked."

I marveled again at how fortunate we were to have Laura-Nicolas and Gerry on the case. Not only were they many steps ahead of us at all times, their connections in Pennsylvania were invaluable.

"Laura-Nicolas and Gerry, after this case is solved you must plan a trip to Engelberg. I know the polizei will want to thank you profusely in person," Dominique added.

"Consider it done, Dominique. This little adventure has put Engelberg at the top of our traveling bucket list!"

After hanging up, Dominique and I spent some time reviewing our conversation with the Völlmers.

"You know, Donna, I am surprised that Hermann and the other officers have still not been able to get any useful information out of Linda/Louise. I know their interview techniques are most effective, but they seem unable to crack this particular nut."

"Maybe you should call Officer Bachmann, and ask if there is anything we can do to help. I would never want to make them feel incompetent, but I'd be so willing to give it a try."

Dominique placed a call and we were invited back to the station for a brief tête-à-tête about the best means of handling Frau Bodner/Bonita.

#####

Once comfortably in our seats in conference room A, we began our discussion.

"Frau Gisin and Frau Leigh, we can understand where you might think we have been too lenient on our captive, but you must understand that we are navigating a delicate situation. To begin with, as a successful undercover agent, Frau Bonita is far more elusive than our average perpetrator. And normally, we would simply throw the book at an individual clearly guilty of passport fraud, but our normal channels have been proving ineffective in this case.

"From the start, Frau Bonita has not been intimidated by any of our declarations of guilt and the ensuing consequences. By the way she throws around the U.S. Embassy, you would think she was a high ranking political official. She also talks of attorneys who will be flying over from the U.S. – and refuses to utter a word in answer to any of our questions until they arrive. During one conversation she even declared her intention of standing behind the Geneva convention, and in all honesty, I believe she genuinely thinks she is involved in an international war. We are at a loss as to our next step."

"Well, here's a thought. Why don't you let Dominique and me talk to her?"

"That would be highly irregular, but we seem to be out of options for the moment. What would you say to her?"

"We would start out by implying that we know far more than we already do."

"And again, we're lying. You know that will be up to you, Donna."

"Yes, Dominique. In the U.S. we just call that good negotiating. We'll drop in a few obvious facts that are vague

243

enough but sufficiently on point to make her begin to doubt her feelings of superiority over authority." This is kind of my thing, I was so in my zone! "And then, once we sense vulnerability, we go in for the kill!"

"And what, pray tell is the kill, Frau Leigh?"

"She spills her guts about Jones and the connection to Will and that will greatly improve her ability to ever get out of a Swiss prison in her lifetime."

"Well, as you Americans say, 'it's worth a shot'."

The next thing we knew, we found ourselves in an interview room with our stalker who was possibly also responsible for attempted murder.

"I don't know who you are, but I have nothing to say to you."

"Sure, we get it. Why would you talk to us? And by the way, I think you do know who we are since you spent some time stalking both of us. So why don't you just drop the BS and confirm what we already know."

"And just what is it that you think you know?"

"We know that you work in pharmaceutical in Pennsylvania. We know that your area of expertise is covert operations also known as corporate espionage. We know that you have hired Beau Jones on several occasions to do the "dirtier" of your dirty work. And we know that this recent operation was focused on the work of Will Bryner."

Linda/Louise was visibly deflating and her face was turning from greenish to gray/green. One of the fall colors of

Sherwin Williams. I could see the effect this transformation was having on Dominique.

"So, Louise, Dominique and I are going to step out for a moment and give this information a chance to sink in. We'll be back in a few."

As soon as the door closed behind us, Dominique began her own interrogation.

"How did, did we, we really didn't know, what the hell was that?"

"That, my friend, was weaving the truth in with a stellar SWAG. No, we don't know at least half of that – for sure. But, come on, at this stage what else could it be?"

We grabbed a quick hot chocolate and headed back into the interview room.

"So, Louise," Dominique began, "one thing I can tell you for sure, the more information you share with us the more cooperative you'll be considered to be, irrespective of your Embassy and your pack of legal counsel."

That was all it took. This canary was ready to sing!

"Look, murder was never the intention. That's all I have to say. Murder should be taken off the table. Our only intent was minor inconvenience. But, if you've done your homework, you know that Jones was a bumbling idiot who messed up anything he touched."

"Then why the hell would you have sent him on this mission?"

At this point, Louise was actually looking sheepish.

"Well, because we didn't really care about the final outcome. We figured whatever he did would cause inconvenience, and we were prepared to accept anything beyond that. Never in our wildest imaginations would we have believed that the idiot could have killed himself and barely impacted anyone else. It's just as well he died because he would never have seen another penny from me! Moron!"

Dominique and I were stunned. Never had we seen such a Laissez faire and downright callous attitude about anything, much less something this potentially dangerous.

"Okay, Louise, that's a very good start. Now, tell us why you were hoping to inconvenience Will."

"I think I've said quite enough. You tell the polizei what I said, and I will await word from my legal counsel."

We left Louise feeling disappointed. We had failed at getting to the bottom of this case.

"You have gotten much further than we," stated Officer Bachmann elatedly.

"Yeah but…"

"No buts. This is very important in helping shape the rest of our focus and our questioning. You got her to admit to illegal intention, to hiring an incompetent to perform her nefarious task, as well as to acknowledge indirectly that Will and his drug were the target. You have achieved far more than you realize and we are grateful."

So all in all, not such a bad day. Maybe we'd treat ourselves to a special dinner tonight.

#####

Dinner that night included Dominique and the Bryners. Talk was divided between our earlier conversation with Louise Bonita and preparations for Lyra's big race in a few days.

Dominique would be doubling up on Lyra's training sessions. I was sure Jon would want to be part of the excitement, so I sort of took stock of what next steps I felt would be necessary in our investigation. We'd have to give the Völlmers some time to conduct their clandestine interviews and there would likely have to be at least one more conversation with Frau Bonita. It appeared as though there would be little to do for at least a few days, leaving me free to spend some time with the training crew as they prepared for the big race, and a bit of time for sightseeing.

After dinner, I dropped a quick email to Laura-Nicolas and Gerry filling them in on our conversation with Louise Bonita. I felt the more we honed the details and closed in on the actual facts, the tighter their interviews could be.

As I finished typing, Dominique appeared with a steaming cup of hot chocolate – so thoughtful. I took a photo and texted it to Barbara in Boston to make up for all the chocolate and hot chocolate stories she had regaled me with over the years. Payback is a bitch!

"I see you are tying up some loose ends, Donna."

"Just trying to keep things moving and myself feeling useful."

"If we can believe the comments from the polizei this afternoon, I don't think we need to keep proving this to ourselves."

"I agree. But I also know Jon and I can't stay here in Engelberg indefinitely, and I think the pressure of 'time through the hourglass' is causing me some added agita."

"Oh yes. I can see where that could be a problem. It is hard for me to think of you and Jon heading back to the U.S. I think I have just put it out of my head and the day of your departure will come as quite a shock. Perhaps there is something I can do to make it feel even more special."

I was quite touched by Dominique's candid admission. As a celebrity she was no doubt used to people coming and going in her life. The fact that our departure would be difficult for her to accept was quite an honor. I couldn't begin to imagine anything she could possibly do that would be better than our countless memorable experiences since we had arrived in Switzerland.

"Dominique, every single day has been special – aside from the whole murder part. Trust us, being able to go to that race in St. Moritz will be special enough."

[Chapter 37]

The next morning Jon left to meet with Dominique and Lyra at Titlis. I felt a leisurely breakfast and some shopping mixed with sightseeing was in order.

As I took my second sip of coffee there was a knock at the door. My heart stopped momentarily. Who could that be?

"Donna, I know you're in there. And you have some things to explain Missy," screeched Clovis through the door.

And just like that, my life flashed before my eyes.

I tiptoed over to the door. Why I felt that stealth would help me was anyone's guess. It's not as though I could come up with something/anything to control the tiny She Devil waiting to pounce as soon as the door was open. I guess it was dread that slowed me down.

"Well, it's about time! And can I just ask you what you thought you and your racing friend were doing yesterday by interviewing the suspect without me? You know very well that I am the brains behind any interviews that you have ever handled well. Okay, you've never handled an interview well, it has always been me!"

The screeching was already giving me a headache. At that moment, I genuinely understood the urge to kill. Thank goodness I'm basically a coward at heart. That was all that saved her. And before I had a chance to utter a word…

"Don't worry. I fixed everything."

I could only imagine.

"I phoned your Officer Hermann Bachmann and explained that you are never and should never be permitted to speak to suspects in an investigation. That you have only ever managed to make things more difficult and confusing. I implored him to give me the details of your interview but he was unable due to regulations pertaining to an ongoing investigation. Clearly, it would take some time for the Swiss police to trust me as well as the U.S. police did."

It was a legitimate strain to keep from rolling my eyes all the way back into my head!

"No matter. I know you well enough to be able to surmise how the interview went. I told him I was certain the suspect had explained she was an executive in a pharmaceutical company but that they certainly never engaged in corporate espionage. I went on to further speculate that she had never met nor had any knowledge of Jones. I made sure Officer Bachmann understood that anything you had determined in your ill-advised interview was unquestionably inaccurate.

"Once I was finished, it was clear I had greatly impressed him. He even said "Frau Seville, your take on the interview in question is quite remarkable." So, I went on to tell him that I am always the one to come up with the real facts in any investigation. I am quite certain they will be releasing Louise Bonita sometime today since she has done nothing wrong. Oh, Donna, don't thank me for cleaning up your mess. It is something I have become quite accustomed to doing."

I congratulated Clovis on her exemplary 'interpretation' of our interview with Bonita and her ability to astound the Swiss polizei with her brilliance. As she stood there glowing, I asked her how she was planning to spend the remainder of the day.

"I will be doing some investigating online and then asking a few questions of my own. And no, Donna, don't ask me to include you in my factfinding mission. You would just slow me down."

And with that, the same ill wind that blew her to my door – blew her out into the unsuspecting Swiss countryside. I felt a small pang of guilt for the Swiss citizens – but I knew they were a tough bunch and could generally take care of themselves. As for Officer Bachmann, perhaps I'd give him a wide berth today – he would still have some open wounds to heal after his recent unpleasant encounter.

#####

After my 'relaxing' morning, I met with Dominique, Lyra and Jon for a late lunch. We spent the first half discussing the morning training session. They were filling me in on the highlights, but, if truth be told, they were discussing amongst themselves and I was nodding on the rare occasion when they looked over at me. That was fine. It was a pleasure to even be only somewhat in the dark when their own excitement was so palpable.

Once the training details were exhausted, I proceeded to fill them in on my visit from Clovis. Then I waited for Dominique's take on things.

"Oh, but, Donna, that's not, that's not, how, I mean…"

"You get used to it."

"But Hermann Bachman?"

"Knew just how to handle her, kudos to him."

"Then you don't think he…?"

"Believed her? No, I don't. I could tell just from what she relayed to me about his end of the conversation that he was adept at handling a highly unstable individual. I'm sure that was part of his training for the polizei. You know, you don't add fuel to the fire, you don't fan the fire, you let the flames die out gently and painlessly.

"He was able to both assuage her fury at me as well as keep any relevant information about the investigation away from her. I'd say his response was masterfully executed. It took the Omaha police a bit longer to successfully handle her Tasmanian personality."

I could see that Dominique too was beginning to fight off a stress headache. You had to give it to Clovis, she could make people sick in person as well as from a distance.

#####

Upon awaking the next morning, I realized that I had received a cryptic text message from the Völlmers.

Herr Bryner was not the intended victim in the attack. It was Lyra!

What? Why? That made no sense. Why would a U.S. pharmaceutical company even care that Will had a daughter named Lyra? Even with the slight bit of attention she'd received for winning a few local races it was highly unlikely that word of her achievements would garner any notice at all among corporate U.S. executives.

And why would anyone want to hurt her? It wasn't like she had been an intern of her Dad's and learned any of the details about the drug he had worked on. Were they just targeting Lyra to get a message through to Will and his employer? And what exactly was that message? I debated mentioning anything about the text until I could get a mental handle on it, but once I spoke with Dominique I couldn't keep something this big to myself.

"Donna, that is terrifying!"

"I know, Dominique. But don't get too upset just yet. I have to believe that, for the first time, the Völlmers have gotten it wrong."

"But Donna."

"I know. I never thought I would utter those words, but anything else is just too horrifying to even consider!"

"I have such mixed feelings. I want them to be wrong, but I sense they would not have sent that text were they not absolutely certain. So, let's agree to keep that to ourselves until we have a chance to speak with them and find out how they reached that conclusion. I have to believe they have additional information that will help us reach our own conclusion."

As usual, Dominique was able to stabilize and contain a potentially highly volatile turn in our investigation. We would have to keep this under wraps until all the details were laid out and the resources were vetted to our satisfaction. Anything less would be irresponsible. We agreed to schedule a call with the Völlmers for as soon as possible.

One thing I knew. Dominique and Jon would be off for even more training with Lyra and I would head out to do some sightseeing – but none of us would have a calm and relaxing day. The Völlmer text had just made everything that much more real and far more terrifying.

#####

I did my best to put aside my frazzled nerves as I ventured in and around more of the stunning treasures of Engelberg. But it was to no avail. I might as well have been watching a documentary from my living room in Omaha for the diminished effect of seeing these lovely sites up close and in person. I would be mad at myself later for allowing my increased anxiety to dampen my ability to fully appreciate such splendor. My mind just kept returning to the now infamous text.

Was Lyra really the target for the mishandled assassination? How could we protect this sweet young girl from a ruthless international industry? Questions just kept flashing into my mind, and there were no answers forthcoming. One thing that did become alarmingly evident the more I thought. We would have to fill the Engelberg police in on this information whether or not we'd spoken with the Völlmers. Lyra needed a protection detail until this investigation was concluded.

I had texted the Völlmers earlier about a good time for a call and had just heard back. They would be occupied with some charity commitments for the next two days which would keep them from being accessible during the times we were available, so they immediately offered to cancel their event. I assured them that regardless of getting anything more from them, we could not wait before sharing our information with the police and finding a way to ensure Lyra's safety. That was priority one!

I was loathe to take this course of action because it would mean having to share this reprehensible news with the whole Bryner family, including Lyra. It made me heartsick to have to scare all of them, but there didn't seem to be any reasonable alternative at this point.

Later that afternoon, I filled Dominique in on the status of the text and what I had concluded were the necessary next steps. She agreed wholeheartedly and placed a call to Hermann to set up a meeting with the polizei. There was no time to lose. Knowing Lyra could have been in danger all this time was a harsh dose of reality.

"Donna, just to keep you in the loop, in addition to our meeting with the polizei, I requested another meeting with Frau Bonita. We may have to wait a few days to speak with the Völlmers, but you can be sure this woman is at the heart of the entire botched escapade. This time we will not be quite so nice. We'll need to plan our script carefully to try to elicit her plans regarding Lyra. She is tricky, but we will need to outsmart this diabolical creature."

"That is exactly right!"

Dominique just smiled. We really did make a great team!

[Chapter 38]

We rushed through an early tea, filling Jon in on our latest information. He just smiled and nodded his head. This was getting old.

After tea, Dominique and I headed over to the station for our meeting with the murder investigation team. Once we'd filled them in, we observed all of their puzzled facial expressions. Apparently, they were undergoing the same thought process we had. The thought of anyone targeting Lyra was beyond all of us. We waited and watched their wheels turning.

Once they had digested our news the murder team, to a man, agreed that Dominique and I needed to get to Bonita ASAP, so we were ushered into an interrogation room with little fanfare. Within minutes, Louise Bonita was escorted in and seated before us.

"Look Louise," I started since maybe the American connection would help in some way, "as disturbing as this whole thing is, we have just uncovered some information that takes it to a whole new level of horrific."

At this comment I could see Bonita stiffen. That would probably not help in getting any kind of admission from her. I had clearly miscalculated thinking a fellow American – especially an east coast American – would respond to our typically blunt approach. Another epic fail, and one that could cost us valuable time in keeping Lyra safe. Maybe I wasn't as good at this detecting thing as I'd led myself to believe. Luckily, Dominique was there to pick up the slack.

"You need to understand, Louise, that we are not accusing you of any more than having some role in this whole curious venture. We understand you may not have been calling the shots and you may not even be privy to all of the details. We are merely asking you to help us fill in some of the gaps so that we can safeguard Lyra or anyone else who may still be at risk."

At that I could see Bonita visibly relax. Not completely, but she no longer looked like a figure in Madam Toussaud's Wax Museum. Way to go, Dominique. Maybe I should let her handle this whole interview. At the very least I would take my cue from her and not try to overwhelm the prisoner.

Dominique looked at me to indicate I was up. Well, if she had confidence I wouldn't blow it – maybe I should too.

As I glanced at Bonita's face, I could see that in addition to being more relaxed, she also managed to look annoyed. Was she angry that Dominique had minimized her role – even though having a lesser role would serve to protect her? Women can be funny creatures – sometimes our egos take a front seat even if that also places us in the 'hot seat!' These days we are programmed to demand recognition for what we've achieved. Even, I guess, if what we achieve is a high profile in infamy.

"So, Louise, can you at least tell us if Lyra was the intended victim?"

After a great deal of hesitation and a lot of looking back and forth between Dominique and me, Louise began to talk.

"You are correct in assuming that my role in all of this was quite minimal." I didn't believe that for a second, but I kept my mouth shut and Bonita continued.

"I am, or was, an executive in a pharmaceutical company in Pennsylvania, Nitra-Droviter." We knew that from our call with the Völlmers and from Engelberg's Miami sister city.

"I was told there were some insignificant elements created by a partnership with a Swiss pharmaceutical that needed some hands on attention, but did not necessarily need a particularly intelligent or high level individual to get them done.

"I had met Jones at a cocktail party and was led to believe he was kind of a corporate Jack of all trades. I mean, a guy who could be relied on to take out the garbage and get it into the right receptacle. He would be cheap and he would take orders. I had no idea of the specifics of the assignment. And frankly, what little I knew of Jones, it was probably a stretch that he could successfully take out the garbage, but it had been described to me as a mission of absolutely no importance, a minor clean up."

Straining to keep from rolling my eyes, and I could detect a similar struggle in Dominique, I ventured a bit further.

"I am curious as to how you could adequately direct Jones if you genuinely knew nothing of the assignment."

Another long pause and Dominique finally jumped in.

"We are most interested in Jones' targeted victim or victims. You are currently being detained as being the primary instigator of this whole tragedy. If you could give us some information that would enable us to protect the target or targets it would go much easier for you. Just because you proclaim to have very little knowledge, does not mean you will be believed. And, should we discover information of your far greater involvement, I hope you will enjoy our prison system for the many years you will be enjoying our Swiss hospitality."

At this Louise turned greenish white and started to hyperventilate. Score another one for Dominique! We suggested she put her head between her knees and gave her a few moments to pull herself together. And then she spoke.

"Okay, okay. I am sincere in telling you that I had only the smallest amount of knowledge, however, within the executive level of any corporation there is always some amount of rumor and gossip, revealing even their deepest, darkest secrets. What I am about to tell you is not something that I could attest to in court – it is merely speculation and gossip that I was either told or that I inadvertently overheard.

"I did overhear that there was to be a target of this mission. But everything I heard through the rumor mill made it very clear that it was to be a minor injury or a serious inconvenience. No one was ever to be killed. I may have been made privy to a bit more information once Jones was found dead and I was sent to complete his mission and erase his footprint to the greatest extent possible.

"One thing was very clear, the death occurred solely due to Jones' incompetence. As I've said before, if you've done your homework you'll know that he was a notorious screw up. And believe me, the top executives at Nitra-Droviter are planning to make me pay for making such a disastrous choice to carry out this mission. Whatever Switzerland has in store for me might be far better than a ruthless U.S. pharmaceutical!"

"This is helpful information, Louise," Dominique conceded, "now what can you tell us about Lyra or any other target? Who should we be protecting?"

"I am less clear on the target, but I have heard Lyra's name mentioned. I only started researching why she might be our intended victim shortly before I was rushed over to Switzerland for damage control, and soon thereafter I landed here in prison. So yes, Lyra was probably the target, but I could not venture to explain why, and I cannot imagine that she, or anyone else, would still be in danger."

She seemed sincere so Dominique and I shared eye contact which agreed we wouldn't push the issue. One thing was for sure though, Lyra was getting a 24-hour guard until we did find out and could put a stop to whatever nefarious Plan B might be in place. So, Dominique took our conversation in another direction.

"Why were you following Donna and me, and clearly trying to 'derail' us?"

"Well, I was told you two were leading the investigation and were getting extremely close to uncovering some seriously damning facts. I felt disarming both of you would slow things down and give us time to determine our best course of action."

That was pretty cut and dry, and it made sense. I felt a rush of relief knowing that this ne'er do well corporate functionary was safely behind bars. All that was left was to ensure that Lyra's guards were posted tout suite.

True to their level of excellence, the Engelberg polizei had assigned a protective guard for Lyra until further notice. They also suggested that Dominique and I accompany them to the Bryner home to explain the reasoning and hopefully to lessen the blow. We were all loathe to terrify the Bryners, but Lyra's safety was what mattered most, so we headed to the Bryner's home in a convoy.

Once the Bryners were briefed on all the latest facts there were, understandably, a few moments of visible fear and grief from the family. Lyra, however, seemed cool and calm. It was clear to see she was taking her cue directly from Dominique. That bond would serve her throughout her racing career and her life.

After a few moments where emotions were allowed to play out, Will cleared his throat and just like magic, calm was restored throughout. That was a neat trick – and one that would never likely work in the U.S. Once again, I had to admire that Swiss stoicism.

From that point on, it was all business. Although it was clear that Lyra was not thrilled about a full-time bodyguard, one look from Papa and all percolating complaints were quelled. I had to learn how to do that.

At this point, Officer Bachmann made a call and moments later a young officer arrived at the Bryner doorstep and was introduced as the first of Lyra's bodyguards. Officer Kroener would be stationed outside of the Bryner house for the first of the eight hour shifts.

Once the plan was fully in place, we said our quiet good-byes and headed to our various destinations. The Bryner's and Dominique agreed to stop by our rental flat in the morning for a continental breakfast before Lyra's final training for the big championship race in St. Moritz in a few days.

[Chapter 39]

Everyone arrived on the early side the next morning as Dominique would use this opportunity to share the details of the St. Moritz race. Since it was such a big deal, we would all attend this final training session to get into the true spirit of the event.

Just as Dominique was about to share details of our convoy to St. Moritz she was interrupted by Jon.

"Dominique, I know this throws a wrench into the works, but sadly, Donna and I will be flying back to the states directly after the race. We have been away from home for so long, our absence is being felt – mostly by Frank, Ellie and their sitters. In fact, we've really pushed the timing. Our sitters have commitments and they can no longer stall the inevitable."

"Well, Jon, this poses a bit of a dilemma. I can think of no way our convoy could get you to the race, and also get you to the Zurich airport in time for your departure. Unless…"

"We're open to any suggestions, unless what?"

"I was hoping to keep this as your surprise, but I think our only chance of getting you to the race in St. Moritz and the Zurich airport on time would be if I were to fly you to both places."

"Seriously, you could do that? That would be a huge thrill!" At Jon's exuberant approval of the plan, I, who had never flown terribly well in a small plane, nor oftentimes in a huge plane, felt myself beginning to turn a slight shade of green. I just nodded mechanically and hoped it would go unnoticed.

"Certainly, I can do that. And frankly, that was something I had planned to do at some point during your visit, it was just that this murder got in the way of pretty much everything else, as you would expect.

"So that's settled then. I will fly Jon and Donna to St. Moritz and then on to Zurich. Will, you'll have to take control of the convoy. Oh, and one thing, guys, it being a small plane, we should be fine with the luggage for your clothing, but we will not be able to fit your skis, they will have to be shipped home in advance." I'm pretty sure my face was '70's appliance avocado green' at this point. I wanted desperately to convey my trust in Dominique, because I did trust her implicitly. But my fear of small planes was running the show.

I remember my first small plane. Jon and I were on our honeymoon and were flying from San Juan to St. Thomas. When the voice on the airport speaker announced we were to walk to the plane single file, my nerves kicked in big time. Thankfully, it was a short journey and the rest of the passengers were seasoned commuters not showing an ounce of concern. Every time the cabin was darkened by a passing shadow – because of the low altitude at which we were flying – I was certain we were goners.

When we finally reached the airstrip in St. Thomas, I began to loosen up just a bit. As soon as the plane stopped, the pilot's door opened. He leaned out, looked at me and said

"Well, I see you made it." Apparently, the commuters and Jon thought this quite amusing.

Dominique just looked at me and smiled. And in that smile I was able to read 'I've got this, you can relax.' And I did – for the moment.

After breakfast we all headed to the mountain. It was a cacophony of voices and people. Apparently, we were not the only ones wanting to attend this, the final training, for the St. Moritz race. Lyra even had several fans who chose to attend the training session since they would be unable to get to St. Moritz for the actual race. And she had some die-hard fans who would attend both in order to cheer her on.

As we stood around looking for some direction, a middle aged woman approached Lyra.

"It is such a thrill to meet you in person! We have been watching your progress and we're so happy to see how well you are doing after your dreadfully debilitating start in life. Our daughter has had some physical challenges of her own and you have been such an inspiration to her! I mean you are the poster child of overcoming disability!"

And that was the moment. Dominique and I looked at one another and we both knew. As Dominique pulled out her phone, she instructed the crowd.

"The training session will be delayed for an hour or so. Donna and I need a brief meeting with the polizei." And Jon just nodded his head.

I was amazed at how quickly Officer Bachmann and his distinguished CO were able to arrive to have a quick confab over what Dominique and I (and apparently Jon) had ascertained.

"There was a woman praising Lyra for her inspirational ability to overcome her physical handicap and rise to accomplish such great athletic feats. It was at this moment when Donna and I both realized the motive behind this entire nightmare.

"You see, as was speculated by our various resources, Nitra-Droviter has made an investment in an inflammation drug – much like the drug that Will Bryner is currently working on." And then I jumped in.

"Even that didn't wave a red flag for us. We know there are many anti-inflammatory drugs already on the market, and surely others being put through their R&D paces."

"But," Dominique continued, "the folks at Nitra-Droviter were less than thrilled when they learned that a major new and improved drug they were about to introduce to the market, after an exceedingly expensive R&D, could witness the enormously expensive introduction they had scheduled flounder before even getting started, thanks to a competing drug from Switzerland.

They had learned that this Swiss drug had accomplished what no other anti-inflammatory drug ever had, even the latest and greatest ones. It had completely cured a young person of her physical ailment, so much so that she had been able to compete as an athlete of rising ability and recognition.

Even though neither drug was indicated for Lyra's rare condition, the recognition she would achieve for her father's anti-inflammatory drug would likely make the major Nitra-Droviter 'mega-splash' more like a ripple in a puddle than the global tidal wave they'd planned. They could not afford to allow her fame and athletic success to compromise their ROI."

"Yes," I added, "they have already spent far too much money on R&D to allow this promising new product to languish. They felt there was no choice but to find a way to keep Lyra from competing, in much the same way that Tonya Harding tried to keep Nancy Kerrigen from competing all those many years ago."

"That's correct, they never intended to kill Lyra. They just happened to hire a profoundly incompetent henchman to carry out their plans."

Once we'd finished our debriefing, the polizei headed out to confirm our speculation and suspicions about Nitra-Droviter's new drug. They assured us that, should all the sophisticated speculation that both they and we had garnered prove to be accurate – it would be time for some long-awaited arrests. And while Bonita would likely end up with some jail time, those top executives waiting to make her pay for her mistake, would surely end up with far more jail time than she.

Dominique and I headed back outside to round up our crew and get this final training session started.

On the way, I texted the Völlmers to let them know we had arrived at the solution thanks in great part to their hard work and clandestine sleuthing. Before we reached our destination Laura-Nicolas texted back:

> *You mean that Nitra-Droviter wanted to render Lyra lame so that the Swiss pharmaceutical would not eclipse the launch of their new miracle drug – the one that has already cost them tens of millions? Gerry had one last interview with a former colleague yesterday. After that we were able to fit all the pieces together and were planning on calling you later today.*

How did they do that?

The day of the big race promised to be bright and beautiful, but for us there was nothing but pitch black as our timing dictated a pre crack of dawn rise. Jon and I grabbed a quick breakfast after packing our bags and setting them by the front door.

We had shipped our skis out the day before, and each of these departing steps was a sorrowful reminder that our time here was finally at an end. True, we missed Frank and Ellie like crazy, but we would miss our newfound family enormously.

As excited as we were to watch Lyra in this race, we knew it would highlight our last moments together – so bittersweet. My sadness had even kept me from obsessing about the upcoming small plane adventure, so maybe it wasn't such a bad thing.

Dominique arrived to drive us to the Kägiswil airfield. I had a momentary flutter of nerves when she mentioned we had to wait for daylight since they had no lights. She also mentioned that we could watch her do her safety check and fill the plane up with gas. It's possible I was a tad nervous to see this illustrious airport. Dominique mentioned that it was lacking any bells and whistles. Did she think that was helping me? It wasn't helping!

On the drive, Dominique filled us in on her early morning conversation with Hermann Bachmann.

"With all their newfound contacts in place, the Engelberg police were able to verify our hypothesis in short order. They had already been in touch with police and FBI in Pennsylvania and had the short list of Nitra-Droviter executives that would likely be spending many years in a Swiss prison. They had also been able to confirm that Bonita was the driving force behind the entire operation and would most certainly never see U.S. soil again.

"And actually, the polizei were somewhat stumped by a line from one of the FBI guys that had all the other U.S. law enforcement officials breaking into a hearty belly laugh. The U.S. official who interviewed the top official at Nitra-Droviter made a comment about poor deceased Jones. He said "to call him stupid would be an insult to stupid people."

Dominique looked puzzled when Jon and I burst into laughter. How many times had we heard Jamie Lee Curtis deliver that line in 'A Fish Called Wanda?' And it never failed to crack us up. That would be on our list of movies to watch when Dominique came to visit us in the states.

So, this was it. It was really over. With all the hype and hysteria this soft conclusion was a bit underwhelming. Don't get me wrong, we were all thoroughly relieved that we had reached a final conclusion and that we could be certain Lyra was no longer in danger, but was it wrong to hope for a more dramatic denouement? Oh god, now I was starting to think like Clovis. If I kept this up I would start to hyperventilate.

"So, Dominique, was there any word on Clovis? I just realized that she has been uncharacteristically quiet for several days now."

"Ah yes, Clovis. Hermann tells me that she decided to direct her 'investigating' skills at the Engelberg polizei. That was not wise on her part. When they found her tampering with some evidence at the crime scene they lost no time in throwing her in jail."

Now I really was hyperventilating – but in a good way. Was it physically possible to hyperventilate and laugh hysterically at the same time?

"Oh crap!" Was the best I could do.

"Indeed. And they only agreed to let her out by providing her with an escort to the airport and a flight back to the states. They tell me her reaction was one for the books."

I could only imagine, everything that woman did was one for the books!

"So, she's gone?"

"That she is. And I would be quite surprised if she didn't choose to lay low for a time. My guess would be you will hear from her in a few months and she will have found a way to blame you for this entire experience. In fact, I would go so far as to say she will not have experienced any humiliation herself

– somehow, that will all have been your personal embarrassment, and she will have tried to warn you but, once again, you will have been too stubborn to acknowledge her superiority, Donna."

"Dominique, your insight into human nature is nothing short of astounding!"

"I would argue that she is pretty easy to read."

"I'm going to stick with astounding."

We arrived at the airport and it was immediately clear that Dominique had not exaggerated. That knowledge caused some of the butterflies to flutter up and slam around in my gut. A few deep breaths should help.

In true businesslike fashion, Dominique sat us down in the office building, and I use that term loosely, on the only two plastic – and slightly cracked – chairs while she went about the business of preparing for our flight.

"Donna, more deep breathing."

Good idea. By the time we began to taxi I would be able to sing an aria from Madam Butterfly. It was time.

Seeing Dominique made me both more confident and more nerve-wracked. We proceeded to board.

I may have blacked out for a moment or two. When I regained my senses there was only one emotion. Sheer wonder at the breathtaking views. After a few minutes in flight, Dominique asked Jon, "Are you ever going to share what you wrote about the solution to the investigation?"

"Actually, Donna, why don't you text Tom. I had Will give it to him to take back to the states just to ensure the highest level of security."

Within minutes I received a response from Tom. It said:

> *Lyra is definitely being targeted. Most likely by a competitive pharmaceutical because her miraculous and heroic story gives Mornovado, Will's employer, such a huge advantage over any U.S. pharmas. It is doubtful the henchman was out to kill her, but they would want to render her unable to race.*

Why do I bother?

"My god, Jon. How is it possible you did not spill any of this during the investigation?" Dominique was stunned. It was her first rodeo.

"I could see that the investigation was heading in that direction, and I knew that all of the legwork you and your cohorts were doing would be necessary in order to launch a trial against a major U.S. pharmaceutical. Had I seen things going astray I would have gently tried to push them back on track. And most importantly, I went out of my way to ensure that Lyra was never left alone and vulnerable in any way at any time.

"Besides, you two are far too stubborn to accept what you haven't uncovered for yourself. When I wrote that paper, you would have scoffed at everything on it."

Absolutely true. And in retrospect, Dominique and I could both recall moments when Jon was employing a gentle push. And then our journey took a slightly different turn.

"Donna, how do you feel about your second trip on the Flüelapas?"

"Where? When?"

"Look down."

Holy cow! There it was, a thousand feet below, that hair-raising, death defying, narrow little road winding up and up through the mountains. But all I could see when I looked down was more spectacular scenery. I was mesmerized. I would never quite see the Flüelapas in the same light again.

And before I could recover from this pleasant surprise, we had arrived at the Samedan Airport outside of St. Moritz. What followed was a flurry of activity as we made our way to Corviglia and the much anticipated race; the Swiss National Championships!

[Chapter 40]

Once at Corviglia we were quickly able to find the various parties making up our group. The racers had arrived the day before or even earlier so they could get a feel for the slopes and get to the mountain at first light this morning.

We were thrilled to finally meet Dominique's sister, Michelle. But even better than that was watching the sheer joy from Lyra as she got to meet another one of her heroes.

Michelle's calm demeanor was astounding. I couldn't imagine how anyone could be that serene before a championship race. One look at Lyra and you could see her vibrating and buzzing around like a hummingbird. I couldn't help but ask Michelle.

"How are you so calm?"

She and Dominique both laughed.

"It's not my first rodeo."

We had not flown in early enough to see Michelle take her first run due to the aforementioned lighting absence at the airport. She had been one of the first to race as she was a top ranked skier. After her first run Michelle was in the top 10.

Although Lyra did not hope for such auspicious results, she would treat this race as the most important of her life. As one of the last to ski in this race, she and Dominique soon headed to the top of the mountain to get Lyra mentally ready to perform.

Michelle asked us, "would you like a glass of champagne before heading over to the viewing area?"

"We wouldn't want to drink in front of you, Michelle."

"No worries, enjoy a glass and we can grab a drink together once the racing is complete."

We politely declined the champagne, promising Michelle we'd more than make up for lost time over the course of the day.

"I can see you are anxious to head to the viewing area. I understand you do not want to miss one second of Lyra's race. Let me get you settled and then I promised to meet up with some friends before my second run."

Michelle headed over to the viewing area with The Bryners and Jon and me in tow. We were buzzing just about as much as Lyra. Once assured we were settled, Michelle headed off – as cool as a cucumber. Impressive.

Although it seemed like an eternity, it was finally time for Lyra to race. Her whole run was almost a blur. I had fingernails before she hit the start gate and none as she cleared the finish line. And I don't even bite my nails, but it was worth ingesting a bit of nail varnish for the thrill of being present on this momentous occasion.

Lyra had placed twenty second which would give her an advantage for the second run. Now we would drink champagne – and there was yet another run for her to go!

We left Dominique and Lyra to their mental preparations. The rest of us headed off to the pub for a champagne toast and a bite to eat. Before our drinks arrived, Michelle, who was calmly sipping orange juice before her final run, had us laughing at some of the comedic racing stories she'd witnessed, but mostly about the 'jerry-esque' antics of her older sister.

For this next race, Lyra would be one of the first to ski. I guess that's how they keep things fair in the world of racing. She looked confident in the starting gate – thank you, Dominique – and she headed down the mountain looking smooth as silk. At the finish line, she slid in with the fastest time. What a thrill! While we knew the top racers were still to come and that score could slip by a huge amount, just seeing her in that coveted range was nothing short of phenomenal. And based on some of Dominique's observations, there was a chance that the upper echelon of skiers would be worn out giving Lyra a better chance of maintaining a place within, or close to, the top 10.

We ran behind the Bryners over to where Lyra stood to let her know that we were all as thrilled as could be. I'm not actually sure she was even able to acknowledge our presence. The shock had not yet worn off. We stood around watching the excitement, never wanting to forget this triumphant moment we shared with her.

Then we were back in the viewing area to watch Michelle in her second run of the day. What a thrill! With no more nails to bite, I took to chewing on the ends of my hair. Disgusting. But what can you do?

She was at the starting gate, and it appeared as though she was singing a jaunty little song, and then like a flash she was through the finish line with a time that placed her firmly on the podium.

When all was said and done, Lyra placed 7th and Michelle placed 3rd – what an epic day!

With a final glass of champagne all around – except for poor Dominique who still had to fly us to Zurich – we celebrated our newfound family and friends. This was truly a banner day. Just as we were ready to head out, a magisterial looking gentleman wearing an official racing ski jacket approached Lyra.

"We have been watching you. Today was a banner day in your burgeoning racing career and I just wanted to be the first to say, 'See you in Sölden, very soon!'"

Wow, just wow! We had no idea who he was, but he sure looked official!

Jon whispered in my ear, "Sölden is the first World Cup race of the season. That's huge. Your cousin is headed for great things!"

Our celebration wasn't long as it was soon time to head back to the plane at Samedan.

The flight to Zurich was relatively uneventful. The euphoria had drained us. Luckily, this was nothing new to our pilot, she was in top form! Between the spectacular scenery and the feelings of exhilaration, I wasn't even a little bit nervous. I know, I couldn't believe it either.

We arrived at Zurich Airport with little fanfare and said our thanks and farewells to Dominique. Although sad, we knew this was to be the first of many trips where we would all spend time together. We agreed there should be no 'goodbyes' just 'bis bald!' or (see you soon!). In fact, I was having trouble imagining any future investigating without Dominique, my new partner in solving crime.

The End

The Donna Leigh Mysteries

Is It Still Murder Even If She Was A Bitch?

I Didn't kill Her But That May Have Been Shortsighted

I Don't Know Why They killed Him; He Wasn't Really That Annoying

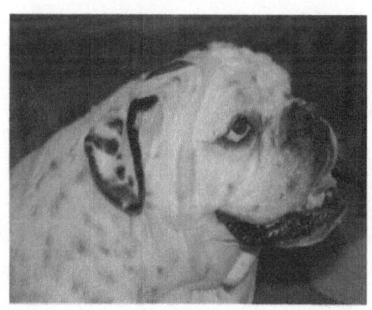

Gracie Dancer LLC

www.rldonovan.com